The
Don Pendleton's®
Executioner®

SHADOW HUNT

D0199194

A GOLD EAGLE BOOK FROM
WORLDWIDE®

TORONTO • NEW YORK • LONDON
AMSTERDAM • PARIS • SYDNEY • HAMBURG
STOCKHOLM • ATHENS • TOKYO • MILAN
MADRID • WARSAW • BUDAPEST • AUCKLAND

Recycling programs
for this product may
not exist in your area.

First edition July 2011

ISBN-13: 978-0-373-64392-9

Special thanks and acknowledgment to
Garrett Dylan for his contribution to this work.

SHADOW HUNT

Printed in U.S.A.

Bolan woke to the hum of a mosquito swarm

His hands and feet were tied together and he was strung up between two willow trees that were slowly bending with his weight. Blood dripped from the cut on his scalp into the water below, carrying his scent to the alligators that infested the area.

He scanned the water for the telltale ripples of an approaching gator and spotted not one, but several, slowly closing in on him. For the moment, Bolan was safe, though it was only a matter of time before the branches gave way.

One alligator was getting more curious, and as it swam around below Bolan, a trickle of blood hit the water. Large jaws snapped out and slashed through the murky swamp.

The tree limbs creaked as Bolan tried to inch his body away from the reptile, and the Executioner knew that his chances of survival were diminishing with every second. Using all his strength, he pulled on the limb that seemed most likely to break. The tree groaned in objection, but finally relented. As the gator surfaced again, Bolan reached up and grabbed the sagging branch. It lowered inch by inch as he struggled to free his arm. The gator swam beneath him, his tail flicking Bolan's boot as a subtle reminder that his time was just about up.

Bolan strained harder at the branch, while watching the gators on final approach. One of them circled and dived below the surface, and Bolan wondered if the creature was going to come leaping out of the water to snatch him in its jaws, like he was a worm on a hook.

The Executioner's premonition proved accurate.

MACK BOLAN ®
The Executioner

Every man has his price...
—English 18th-century proverb

There may not be much in this world that comes free,
but there is one thing that nobody can put a price on—
human life. And I will challenge anyone who tries!
—Mack Bolan

THE
MACK BOLAN
LEGEND

Nothing less than a war could have fashioned the destiny of the man called Mack Bolan. Bolan earned the Executioner title in the jungle hell of Vietnam.

But this soldier also wore another name—Sergeant Mercy. He was so tagged because of the compassion he showed to wounded comrades-in-arms and Vietnamese civilians.

Mack Bolan's second tour of duty ended prematurely when he was given emergency leave to return home and bury his family, victims of the Mob. Then he declared a one-man war against the Mafia.

He confronted the Families head-on from coast to coast, and soon a hope of victory began to appear. But Bolan had broken society's every rule. That same society started gunning for this elusive warrior—to no avail.

So Bolan was offered amnesty to work within the system against terrorism. This time, as an employee of Uncle Sam, Bolan became Colonel John Phoenix. With a command center at Stony Man Farm in Virginia, he and his new allies—Able Team and Phoenix Force—waged relentless war on a new adversary: the KGB.

But when his one true love, April Rose, died at the hands of the Soviet terror machine, Bolan severed all ties with Establishment authority.

Now, after a lengthy lone-wolf struggle and much soul-searching, the Executioner has agreed to enter an "arm's-length" alliance with his government once more, reserving the right to pursue personal missions in his Everlasting War.

Prologue

U.S. Marshal Jack Rio did his best to get comfortable in the too small seat of the rental car. He wasn't muscle-bound or obese, but he had broad shoulders and stood a few inches over six feet tall. With the exception of a full-size truck or an SUV, not too many vehicles on the road were made for someone his size, so getting in and out of the black Nissan Sentra for him felt like he was getting in and out of a clown car. On the seat next to him was a slender briefcase, and his sweat-stained cowboy hat that had about as much business in New Orleans as he did.

Rio pulled another cigarette out of his hard pack, lit it and blew the smoke out the open window. He tossed the remaining pack into the console and mentally reminded himself that he should quit when he got back home. Overhead, the sky threatened rain, but so far as he'd seen, it did that almost every day here. Maybe it was the season, he thought, but it was no wonder the city worried about floods and hurricanes—if it was any lower, it'd been *under* the damn Gulf, not next to it.

The door to the restaurant he was watching opened, and he tensed, then relaxed as a young couple came out holding hands, laughing, and headed for their car. Mosca's was busy this night, and despite its nondescript white exterior and plain sign, the food was reputed to be outstanding.

The fact that it had been the epicenter of organized crime in the area until the early nineties hadn't apparently done much to harm business. New Orleans was really the beginning of organized crime that started with two Matranga brothers in the late 1800s and ended with the last-known leader of the Matranga Family, Carlos Marcello. He died in 1993, but he'd worked out of Mosca's as much as anywhere. Which made the whole damn situation that Rio was in even more strange.

The marshal shifted in his seat, flicked ash out the window, and tried to ignore the trickle of sweat that slid free of his short-cropped black-and-gray hair and down the center of his back. Everyone in New Orleans was sweaty. It was always hot and humid, just on the edge of raining. Under his navy blue sport coat, his .45-caliber Smith & Wesson was heavy and uncomfortable, molding his dress shirt permanently into his skin, but there was no way he was going to take off the coat—or the gun. A lot of experienced shooters carried a 9 mm pistol for personal protection, but Rio's experiences as a U.S. marshal had taught him the value of a weapon powerful enough to a blow a hole in an engine block.

Rio believed in many things, but the existence of both true evil and pure human fuckery convinced him to load his .45 magazine with hollowpoint rounds, and to carry the weapon at all times when he was awake and have it close at hand when he was asleep. So far, his approach had kept him alive in spite of assignments hunting down very bad men from Mexico to California and all over the American Southwest: Texas, Arizona, New Mexico and even southern Nevada. As a "floater" for the U.S. Marshals Service, Rio traveled wherever the higher-ups decided they wanted him to go, working on cases ranging from missing persons to drug runners to vicious killers that they'd prefer the media never heard about.

Sighing, Rio opened the door of the rental car and climbed out, continuing to watch the restaurant. The entire situation *felt* wrong, and his instincts weren't something he took lightly. Why in the world would that shine boy from the DA's office want to meet here? He had to know that Marcello had been using this same restaurant as a front and a meeting place back when he was running things down here. Maybe the attorney just had a twisted sense of humor, but that didn't quite fit, either.

The real bitch of it was that he was totally on his own here. This wasn't an official case, and he sure as hell wasn't on duty. He was supposedly on vacation, but like some other law-enforcement officers he knew, there were no real vacations for him—just times when he worked a case out of his jurisdiction because it smelled funny and he wanted to try to figure it out. That's why he was here, sweating through his shirt and his sport coat, instead of drinking cold beer and fishing in the Gulf with his brother.

Almost a year ago, when he was running down a fugitive who'd thought he could hide out in L.A., Rio had met an old FBI hound who talked about the organized crime in New Orleans and how their whole operation just kind of vanished after Marcello died. It stank to high heaven, but no one had been able to find anything else that could establish they were still there and still in business. Rio had been intrigued, and did a little digging of his own. Over time, organized crime in New Orleans had gotten into all of it: drugs, smuggling, money laundering and the usual organized crime list of dirty deeds, and the Matranga Family was in charge of it all.

Usually, when an organized crime family went out of business, it was because another family came in and took over, or everyone was killed, but so far as the Feds could tell, organized crime was out of business entirely in the New Orleans area.

And since the whole damn city was corrupt, Rio thought, that didn't make one thin dime's worth of sense.

Someone was there—it was just a question of finding them out. Since Rio's main job was locating people who didn't want to be found, he figured he'd go down and spend a week poking around. At the time, he'd thought something might turn up simply because he was an outsider and could see things a bit differently than a local. So far, however, he'd run into a lot of shrugged shoulders, dead ends and urban stories that were more legend than fact. Until he'd spoken to the kid from the DA's office, Trenton Smythe, Rio had pretty much figured that he was going to come up as empty as everyone else.

He took one final drag on his cigarette and tossed it to the ground, crushing it beneath his boot heel. Something didn't feel right, but he was supposed to be on a plane home tomorrow, so if he was going to find anything, he had to find it now. And in spite of his smarmy name and nervous manner, Smythe had seemed convinced he knew something worth telling. Since it appeared he'd run out of options, Rio crossed the parking lot and entered the restaurant.

Smythe was sitting in a booth near the back, his tie loosened and his brown hair mussed, which seemed unusual to Rio. He pegged him as the polished type who looked down on anyone who wasn't wearing a pressed suit and tie, like the first time Smythe saw Rio in the DA's office. But the young attorney didn't look polished this night with his yellow shirt unbuttoned at the top and looking like it had been slept in. An unopened bottle of wine and two glasses, waited on the table, along with a couple of menus. Even though the bottle of wine wasn't open, Rio would wager his pension that Smythe had already had a drink or two. When Smythe spotted Rio, he raised a hand in greeting. As the marshal walked across the restaurant, he noticed that most of the tables were full and waiters scurried back and forth with food and wine. Nothing appeared out of place.

As he reached the table, Smythe stood and said, "I didn't think you were coming. You're late."

"I'm cautious," Rio said. "I've been here for a half hour, just watching."

"For what?" he asked.

"Trouble," he replied. "Trouble's like reality—it shows up when you least expect it."

Smythe shrugged noncommittally. "Wine?" he offered, holding up the bottle. Rio didn't know much about wine, but the aged merlot seemed like a big gesture for someone on government pay.

"No, thanks," Rio said. "You go ahead."

A waiter appeared at the table, opened the wine and poured. After telling them the specials, he asked for their order. Rio ordered spaghetti and Smythe the house shrimp specialty, then the waiter headed off for the kitchen to turn in the ticket. No matter what else, the smells coming from the kitchen were enticing.

After a minute or two of silence, Rio decided to nudge Smythe a bit. "So," he said. "You told me you had information about organized crime in this area after Marcello died. Why don't you share it with me?"

Smythe scoffed. "That's easy?" he asked. "You're not any smarter than the other federal law officers in this area."

Rio held up his hands in mock surrender. "You're the one who said you had information. I'm just asking what it is."

"Well, nothing's free," Smythe retorted. "Hell, they're charging for air at the gas stations now, and if I tell you what I know, I've got to get something for it, too."

The waiter returned, refilled the wineglasses and set out

bread on the table. "Your meals will be up in a couple of minutes."

Once he'd left, Rio said, "What do you want?"

"Two things," he said. "First, I want out of New Orleans—out of Louisiana—and I mean way out. Fucking Wyoming or Canada or something."

Knowing what was coming, Rio asked anyway. "And?"

"A boatload of cash," he said. "Enough so I never have to work a day in my life again."

"So, you want Club Med witness protection," Rio said. "You're dreaming, kid. The FBI's been down here digging for years and found nothing, so whatever you've got can't be that good."

"You don't get it, do you, Rio? No one finds them because they're everywhere—every law-enforcement agency, every cop, every lawyer. The FBI hasn't had any success because their agents are either on the take or kept out of the loop. What I know—what I'll tell you—will rock this city from the top down. It's worth what I'm asking."

"You're going to have to give me more than empty words and promises, boy. I can't just make a call and get you what you want. I'm going to need to have rock-solid evidence—names, places, you name it. And then, maybe."

"What I don't have," he said, "I can get. There are people who trust me, and I have access to everything that I need."

"When?" Rio asked.

"I can have it for you by tomorrow. I just have to copy the files." Smythe took a long swallow of wine, which was when Rio noticed that his hands were shaking.

He took another long look around the restaurant, but didn't see anything that raised his hackles. Still… "You nervous, Smythe?"

"Hell, yes, I'm nervous," he snapped, his blue eyes darting around the room. "Wouldn't you be?"

Rio shrugged. "I'm not the type."

"If you knew these guys, you would be. If they knew I was having dinner with a federal agent, I wouldn't make it through the night," he said. He refilled his glass. "I'll have everything for you tomorrow, but I want your word that you can get me what I want."

Rio thought about it for a moment, then nodded. "I can get it," he said. "But not until I see what you're putting on the table."

"Fair enough. When?"

"First thing in the morning," he said. "My hotel, seven sharp. I've got a flight scheduled to leave at ten."

"You're leaving?" Smythe asked, incredulous. "Now?"

"Relax," Rio said. "If you bring me real information we can use to ferret these bastards out, I'll reschedule."

"Oh, all right, then."

Their food came and they ate in silence. Italian wasn't his favorite, but even Rio had to admit that his spaghetti was very good. He finished quickly, then stood up. "You're buying, right, Smythe?" he asked.

"Sure, sure," he said. His words were slightly slurred, but then he'd almost polished off the entire bottle of wine himself.

"Tomorrow morning, then," Rio said. "Don't be late."

"I won't," he said.

Rio left the restaurant without another word. The parking lot was dark, and his car was parked on the far edge of the lot. He moved with easy grace to the vehicle, sweating already in the humid night air. He unlocked the door, opened it and wedged himself into the seat. Then he put the key into the ignition, started the engine and reached for the air-conditioning. It was too damn humid to not run it on full blast, and he twisted the dial as far to the right as it would go.

As the vents blasted air into his face, two things happened at once. He recognized the acrid tang of pepper spray, and four large men appeared around his car—one at each door. Almost instantly blinded, he tried the door, but the goon standing there held it shut.

"Damn it!" he said, sneezing, coughing and hacking. He forced himself against the door with all his strength and it popped open. He fell out onto the concrete, reaching for his gun even as he landed. Blind, he didn't have much of a chance, but he wouldn't go down without a fight.

"Don't bother, cowboy," a voice said in his ear. He felt the cold metal barrel of a gun pushed against his flesh.

Still coughing, his lungs and eyes burned from the pepper spray, Rio moved his hands away from his coat. The man pulled out the .45 and handed it to one of his pals. The marshal couldn't make out faces clearly through the tears running from his eyes.

"What the hell?" Rio started to say, when the Italian leather boot slammed into his head.

"Welcome to New Orleans, cowboy," the man said. "The boss wants to have a word with you, and I suggest you cooperate. The gators are hungry this time of year."

Knowing that if he fought now, they'd just kill him outright, Rio relaxed. He'd have to wait for a better opportunity.

"Told you I'd bring him," he heard Smythe's voice say. "Didn't I?"

"Yeah, Trenton, you did real good," the man said.

His eyes were clearing, and Rio saw a man dressed in an expensive suit, Smythe standing behind him. Rio spit blood from his split lip. "I won't be forgetting this, Smythe," he said. "Not for a long, long time."

"You've got more to worry about than I do, *Marshal*. A lot more."

Rio was about to reply when the boot hit him again, this time connecting with his temple, and the world went hot, then dark.

1

There weren't that many people who could call Mack Bolan, aka the Executioner, out of the blue and get an instant response, but Hal Brognola was one of them. Apparently one of the big Fed's colleagues, Jacob Rio—a man Brognola had a great deal of respect for—had become quite concerned lately for the welfare of his brother, U.S. Marshal Jack Rio.

According to Jacob, Jack was almost a week overdue for a visit they'd scheduled. Jacob had told Brognola that his brother had been slated for a couple of weeks off, and they'd planned to use one of them to go fishing in the Gulf. Brognola had asked him what his brother was doing for the other one, but Jacob hadn't known for sure.

"He just said he wanted to check something out," he'd said. "For him, that usually means a really cold case or something way off the beaten path or both."

"You've tried all his numbers?" Brognola had asked. "Gone to his house? Contacted his office?"

"All of the above," Jacob said. "No one knows anything, and it's not like Jack to just disappear."

Trusting Jacob Rio's instincts, Brognola contacted Bolan and relayed the details as he knew them. Bolan caught the next flight to Houston out of Denver, where he'd been taking some downtime mountain climbing. From Houston, the drive down to Galveston where the marshal lived wasn't very long, and Bolan cruised the street looking for the white, two-story house that Brognola had told him Rio called home. He ran through his conversation with Brognola again as he drove. It would seem by all accounts that Rio was the real thing—a tough fighter, a more than competent lawman, and the kind of person you'd want watching your back when all hell broke loose. He wasn't the kind of man to take off on a whim without telling anyone.

Rio's neighborhood was that in name only. It might be an area that would make your average suburban family nervous, as the houses were interrupted by equipment and buildings for the oil companies. It wasn't an area where people would let their kids play on the street.

As the driveway came into view, Bolan saw that a black Lincoln Town Car occupied it, so he pulled up short and parked. There was no record of Rio owning a Town Car in the information that Brognola had sent him. The license plate was Louisiana, not Texas, and wasn't a law-enforcement plate. The Executioner climbed out of the car and eased the door closed, then made his way along a low hedge that fronted the house. He could see that the door was open, but wasn't close enough yet to hear anything from the inside. It didn't help that the ocean was less than two blocks away and the incoming tide was making enough noise that hearing anything that wasn't up close and personal would be difficult.

Deciding that a direct approach might work just as well as stealth, Bolan straightened and turned up the walk that led to the front door. When he neared it, he could hear the sound of muttered cursing and the crash of drawers being slammed shut. He knocked loudly on the door, and called out, "Hey, Rio, you in there?"

The sounds from the back of the house stopped. A long

moment of silence, and Bolan called out once more. "Rio, you in there?"

Hurried footsteps moved through the house, and Bolan saw a man enter the small living room. He was dressed in a nice suit, obviously tailored, but looked disheveled. The coat and shirt were both wrinkled, and his hair was mussed and sweaty. "Sorry, sorry," the man said. He had a distinct accent that marked him as a native of New Orleans. "I was in the back cleaning up." He gestured with a thumb toward the back of the house.

"Yeah, I heard," Bolan said. "I'm looking for Jack Rio. He around?"

"No, uh, he's not here right now," the man said. "Who are you?"

"Oh, just an old friend," he said, stepping into the foyer. "We do a little fishing from time to time, and I thought I'd drop by and see if he was up for something this weekend."

"Fishing, huh?" the man said. He was large enough to fill the entryway into the living room, and he stepped forward to meet Bolan. "You don't look like much of a fisherman."

"These aren't my fishing clothes," Bolan replied, easing the front door shut behind him.

"Yeah, right, whatever," the man said. "Look, Rio's not here, so why don't you beat it?"

Bolan closed the final distance between them, stopping just a couple of steps away from the man. "Sorry," he said, "but I can't do that."

"Why the hell not?" the man demanded. "Come back later."

"Because," Bolan said, jabbing a fist into the man's solar plexus, "I've decided I don't like you."

The man doubled over, but was smart enough to back away at the same time, so Bolan's follow-up missed. He straightened, coming up with a mean-looking .45 from beneath his coat. "Don't take another step," he said, trying to catch his breath.

Bolan didn't hesitate. He stepped in close, even as the goon started to speak, and caught his right arm in a reverse lock with his left. He jerked up hard and felt the elbow snap. The man screamed, and the gun hit the wooden floor with a dull thud. Pushing forward with all his weight, Bolan brought his right hand around and drove a hammer blow to the man's jaw.

He staggered and started to go down. Knowing that his adversary was likely to recover quickly, Bolan chopped a blow into the back of the man's neck. He dropped like a sack of cement.

Bolan moved quickly, yanking a lamp cord out of the wall along with the lamp, using it as a makeshift rope to tie the thug's hands behind his back. It took most of the soldier's not inconsiderable strength to get the thug propped upright against the couch. The man groaned, already stirring.

Leaving him for the moment, Bolan gathered up the dropped .45, noting even as he put it in a pocket that its serial numbers had been filed clean. He jogged toward the back of the house and saw that Rio's office was completely trashed. Drawers were pulled open and tossed on the floor, and the contents of two filing cabinets were spread out everywhere. The computer was on, but only showed a log-in screen.

"What have you gotten yourself into, U.S. Marshal Rio?" Bolan muttered before turning back to the living room.

He pulled a chair from the kitchen table into the living room, turned it around, then retrieved a glass of cold water for himself, and one for the unidentified, groggy man. He returned to the living room, took a drink from his own glass, then poured about half of the other over the man's face. The thug spluttered and came around.

"Welcome back," Bolan said. "I have some questions."

"Yeah, well, you know what you can do with your questions," he said. "I ain't saying anything to you."

"I was hoping you'd feel that way," Bolan said. He leaned back in the chair, tilting it up, then brought it down full force into the top of the man's exposed feet. The bones cracked and popped, and the man screamed for several long seconds.

"Who are you, you fuck? You're not just a buddy!" He was breathing heavily.

"I'm the one asking the questions. Who are you? Who do you work for? And where is Jack Rio?"

"I'm the Tooth Fairy," he said. "I work for Santa Claus and the Easter Bunny. And Jack Rio's in hell."

"Wrong answer," Bolan said calmly. He leaned back in the chair, driving the tips of the legs into the man's feet again. Thankfully, Rio's house was quite some distance from any others, though if the man got much louder, a gag would be necessary.

When he finally quieted, Bolan took a long drink of water. "You need to understand," he said. "I'm only going to ask one more time, then I'm going to lose patience and start hurting you. Up to this point, I've been gentle. So, who are you? Who do you work for? Where's Jack Rio?"

The man looked like he was thinking about another smart-ass remark, but then thought better of it. "I'm Tony Salerno," he said, his voice weak from his screams. "I work for the Family in New Orleans, which is where I last saw your buddy Jack." He shrugged. "I'm guessing he's dead by now."

Family, Bolan thought, the magic word that meant Mafia. But last he'd heard, the Matrangas were out of business in New Orleans. "What Family?" he asked.

"Mine, you mook," he snarled.

"Well, at least I know who to look up when I get there,"

Bolan said. "For their sake, the marshal had better be alive."

"I don't know who you are, but if you go down there looking for Family trouble, you're as good as dead already."

"You'd be surprised how often I've heard that," Bolan replied, taking the man's .45 out of his pocket. "Anything else you'd like to tell me? A good address would help." He knew what the answer would be.

"I'll die first," the man spit. "I'm a stand-up guy."

"Yeah, right," Bolan said as he pocketed the thug's gun. "How about we just let the cops deal with you when they get here. I'm sure there are a few outstanding warrants on you."

In the distance, Bolan heard approaching sirens. Apparently the closest neighbors had heard the screams. Bolan wiped down the chair and glasses, leaving them in the sink.

"Hey, buddy, I hope you got your funeral planned, if you're thinking of going near the Family," the thug said.

Bolan ignored the man—his mind was already moving forward. If he got lucky, he could catch a late flight to New Orleans and look up the newest Mafia Family to call the city home. The Executioner went back outside and made his way to his car—carefully plotting his next move.

NIKOLAI AGRON PAUSED and checked his appearance in the mirror one last time. The look was only one small part of his disguise here, but people tended to believe what they saw, and in him, they saw a perfectly groomed Italian man. He pulled out all of the stops for his look, perfectly tailored Italian suit, shoes from Milan and he even had monogrammed silk handkerchiefs for formal occasions. But on this day he had a more casual look—loose fitting shirt, Dockers and loafers. He'd been down in New Orleans since just after Hurricane Katrina hit, introducing himself around the city as

Nick Costello. His bona fides checked out because he'd been building them for several years.

Nikolai was about as Italian as George Washington. He'd been born in Moscow, worked his way up in organized crime there, and when things began to go to hell, he changed tactics. He taught himself how to become someone else, and he spent years developing several different identities in organized crime families around the world. When Katrina hit, Nikolai—*Nick,* he reminded himself—saw a golden opportunity. New Orleans had been all but free of seriously organized crime since Carlos Marcello, the last of the Matranga Family, had died. For a clever man, this vacuum could be exploited.

So Nikolai Agron disappeared and Nick Costello was born. He established himself quickly and invested in real estate as fast as he could. He made backroom deals, robbed Peter to pay the proverbial Paul, and landed every Federal Emergency Management Agency—FEMA—contract he could get his hands on, and the ones he didn't get he made sure went south in a hurry for the other bidder. All that reconstruction work, which was still going on, provided a great cover for money laundering and smuggling, and the town was quickly learning that no projects moved forward without Mr. Costello's permission. He was already a very wealthy man, and before he was done, he'd have enough money to pay back his enemies in Russia, with interest, and buy a nice, private island to retire on.

There was a discreet tap on his door. "He's ready, boss," a voice called from the other side.

Nick crossed the room and opened the door to see the stern face of Victor Salerno. Salerno was the real thing, born in Italy into a prominent Mafia Family. But he'd long since put profit above honor. As Nick's capo, Salerno knew almost everything about the operation he was running, but he did his best work as an enforcer.

"He's in the game room?" Nick asked, as they descended the steps to the first floor.

"Yeah," Salerno said. "All ready to go."

"Good," Nick said. "He'll talk soon."

"It doesn't matter. Tony will find something that will give us what we need."

"Have you heard from him yet?" Nick asked.

Salerno shook his head. "No, but he'll get in touch soon. He's a good kid."

"Absolutely," Nick agreed. They crossed the main floor of the house to the kitchen, then opened a small door in the back, which revealed a short set of concrete steps leading into the so-called game room—the place where Salerno questioned those who had information he wanted.

The game room wasn't large—perhaps twenty feet on a side—and constantly smelled of wet, mildew and blood. And a carefully trained nose could pick out the scents of urine, feces and, most of all, fear. Jack Rio was chained to a stainless-steel table in the middle of the back wall. Salerno saw that he was awake and staring at him with hatred in his eyes.

"Are you ready to begin again, Mr. Rio?" Nick asked. "I'm enjoying our sessions together."

"You're accent sounds funny to me," Rio said. "What part of Italy are you from?"

Nick made a sad tsking sound between his teeth. "As I've already explained to you, Mr. Rio, I ask the questions here in the game room, not you." He removed a rubber apron from a hook on the wall, hung his suit coat in its place and put on the apron. Then he lifted a metal tray from the shelf and selected a long, thin-bladed device.

"I think we'll start with this," he said, his voice growing quiet. "Unless you'd like to tell me what I want to know."

"You'd best get to cutting," Rio said between his gritted teeth. "Because I'm not telling you shit."

"As you request," Nick said, bringing the blade down and cutting into the delicate skin of Rio's inner thigh. "I'm always happy to play in the game room."

2

Bolan had traveled the world, and that included New Orleans. He'd been there before, and there were two things he knew without a doubt. First, that if the heat and the mosquitoes didn't kill you, the alligators would. Second, behind the Cajun-flavored drawl, there wasn't a single cop in the city who liked having anyone else horn in on their territory.

After arriving on a late flight and tracking down a hotel of very questionable quality, Bolan decided early the next morning to visit the district attorney's office. It was possible that Rio had checked in there, or perhaps word had come through that there was a U.S. marshal in town. Bolan drove his small rental car through the early-morning humidity and parked it across the street from the DA's office. There was a small bistro serving Turkish coffee and scones, and with time to kill until the office opened, Bolan ordered both and sat at a table to wait. The coffee was excellent, and the scones helped to satisfy his hunger, even as his eyes took in the arriving staff and lawyers, who already looked uncomfortable in their business attire that clung to them with the heavy humidity.

The office was located only a couple of blocks from the Louisiana Superdome, where the New Orleans Saints played football. It was a somber-looking building, with a dark gray fabricated granite facing. But the courthouse and other older buildings on the block offered a different atmosphere than the DA's office. Statues and columns, along with honeysuckle vines in the park, lent itself to the old-world feel that New Orleans was famous for. When his watch read eight o'clock, Bolan finished the last of his coffee and walked across the street. By the time he arrived, he was already sweating through his clothing, and even the blast of air-conditioning didn't seem to do much more than make him feel damper. He took the elevator up several floors to where the DA's office was located.

"Can I help you, sir?"

The blonde woman at the front desk was devouring him with her eyes. Her red sleeveless dress plunged in the front, leaving little to the imagination. She leaned forward even further, squeezing her elbows into her sides so that her cleavage all but jumped out and said hello.

Resisting the urge to pull the clinging shirt away from his skin, Bolan turned enough for her to see the badge and gun on his belt. He needed to find Rio in a hurry, and he really didn't want to waste time with someone who was more interested in flirting than being helpful.

"Matt Cooper," he said. "U.S. Marshal's Service, to see the district attorney."

Eyeing his gun carefully, she stammered, "Oh, y-yes, sir. Right away."

He watched her hurry away from the desk, then duck into an office. He hadn't had time to put together a full cover, so using a U.S. marshal's badge was the best idea he could come up with on short notice. It would get anyone in the law-enforcement community's attention, and it cut down on unwanted questions. U.S. marshals worked all over the country, dealing with everything from basic immigration to drug running to federal warrants.

He waited patiently, trying to hear the frantic whispers behind the closed door, but having to be satisfied with the knowledge that things were moving along. After a couple of minutes, the busty woman hustled back out, with a man close on her heels. The sign on the door read District Attorney, but Bolan knew in a minute this guy wasn't the head honcho. For one thing, he was wearing an off-the-rack suit and for another, he was too young.

Bolan watched the small man straighten his shirt and tie, then march forward.

"You gave my secretary a good scare, Marshal Cooper. What's the big idea?"

Bolan stood a little straighter as the man began to talk. The reprimand he was trying to give was weakened with the small quaver in his voice and the fact that he couldn't seem to keep his hands still.

"I don't know why she'd be scared. I let her see my badge, then she went to get you. We're all supposed to be on the same side, right? Can we talk in your office? It's vital that I speak with the district attorney."

"Well, sir, he's not here and won't be before the end of the week. He's at a conference in Washington. Might I suggest that you make an appointment for Monday?"

Bolan looked over the fidgeting man. "You the assistant DA?"

"Yes, yes, I am," he said. "I'm in charge of this office until he returns. Trenton Smythe." He offered a hand, which Bolan ignored.

"Then you'll have to do."

Bolan could see the sweat bead on the little man's brow. He couldn't have been over five-four, and a 130 pounds soaking wet. He looked like an overworked, underweight terrier. If Bolan hadn't been watching so closely, he would have missed the catch in the man's breathing, but not the look in his eyes that said more than any one person could with words. That "Ah, crap," look that was unmistakable.

"Of course," Smythe said finally.

He turned and walked into the office. Bolan nodded to the secretary as he walked past her desk. The outer office was modern and had clearly been updated recently, but the inner office was typical old Louisiana, dark wood paneling, deep rich carpeting and plaques that showed the DA's latest and greatest fishing accomplishment. Mr. Smythe sat confidently behind the DA's hijacked desk.

"Now how can I help you, Marshal?"

"There was a U.S. marshal visiting on his vacation here. He's a friend of mine and has come up missing. I thought I'd check in and see if you had heard anything. His name is Jack Rio."

Smythe pursed his lips. "No…" he said, thinking. "I haven't heard of Marshal Rio, but of course many people come here on vacation. If he wasn't working, why would he check in with us? Are you certain he came to New Orleans?"

Bolan nodded. "I'm sure he came here," he said. "And as for a vacation, well, you know some of us in law enforcement don't really vacation. From what I've heard, he came out this way to look into something on his own time. He's not the type to just go missing."

"Does he have a wife screaming for him or something?"

"No, but he's my friend and I know he was working on something here."

"Ah, I see," Smythe said. He chuckled weakly. "A cold case or something?"

"I don't know for sure," he said. "But if he was following a trail out this way, I figure he might have checked in with your office. It's at least odd that he's gone missing in your jurisdiction."

Smythe stood and went to the door. He peeked out around it before closing it firmly, then returned to the desk. Bolan hadn't even been in the room with the guy five minutes and he wanted to shoot him. It was obvious he knew something about Rio, and Bolan wasn't a patient man.

"You said your friend's name was Jack Rio?"

"That's right."

Smythe began to fidget with the antique pen that was sitting in an inkwell. He leaned back against the desk and stared at Bolan, but his entire demeanor had changed into something more cocky and confident. The soldier sensed this man was more than he appeared and at least part weasel.

"Yeah, all right, now that I think about it, we did have a fella by that name come through here." He glanced suggestively at the door. "But maybe this isn't the best place to be talking about it."

"Look, Mr. Smythe, this is a missing federal agent. If you have some information, you need to tell me. If I don't come up with some answers pretty damn fast, you're going to end up with every federal law-enforcement agency in the country breathing down your neck."

Smythe pulled one hand out of his crossed arms and pointed a stubby finger at Bolan.

"Marshal Cooper, this is New Orleans and down here we do things a bit differently. We don't rush things that we shouldn't rush, and this is one of them. Since Katrina, about all we've dealt with is the Feds, and most of 'em couldn't find their ass with two hands, a flashlight and a map."

Despite the man's attitude, Bolan could tell that Smythe was nervous about something. So he simply sighed and nodded.

"It's your town," he said. "What do you have in mind?"

"That's smart, Marshal Cooper. Why don't we meet around seven over at Mosca's? I'll have more for you then."

"Where might that be?"

"Oh, you'll have found it by seven. It's practically famous. Just ask around, and you'll find it."

A discreet knock on the door interrupted Smythe, and the secretary stuck her head in the door when he called out, "Enter."

"I'm sorry to interrupt you, sir, but Chief Lacroix is here to see you," she said.

A heavily muscled man in a police uniform pushed past her. "Jeezus pleezus, Sally, since when do I need an announcement?"

He stopped as he crossed the threshold and spotted Bolan. "I apologize, Trenton," he said. "I had no idea you were in a meeting."

Bolan stood and moved away from the two men. The officer's name tag revealed that his first name was Duke, and more than anything else, he radiated danger. The soldier wanted room to maneuver in the event he had to make a quick exit. New Orleans had a reputation for being corrupt, especially the police department, and while he wasn't yet sure who was involved in Rio's disappearance, he'd wager his favorite Desert Eagle that at least someone from the police department was involved. And Smythe obviously knew more than he was letting on.

The way Lacroix ignored Smythe told Bolan a great deal about who had the upper hand in their relationship. "Who's this now, Trenton?"

"Matt Cooper," Smythe said. "A U.S. marshal."

"Is that so?" Lacroix asked. "What brings you to the DA's office, Marshal?"

"I'm here investigating the disappearance of another marshal," Bolan replied evenly. Lacroix was dangerous—Bolan felt that as clearly as he'd feel it from a water moccasin.

"It's common courtesy for you boys to check in with

the locals before you conduct any investigation in someone else's jurisdiction. I'm sick of you *federales* thinkin' you can come in here as pretty as you please without a little common courtesy."

"Oh, you were next on my list," Bolan said. "As soon as I was done here."

"Is that so?" Lacroix said, using the same expression of doubt again. "What's the name of your missing marshal? I haven't heard of anything coming our way, and we usually get a flash alert on those kinds of things."

"He was off-duty," Smythe offered. "Supposedly, he was down here on vacation, but he's gone missing."

"Huh," the police chief said. "Sounds like you're wasting your time, Marshal Cooper. He probably hooked up with some sweet thing and is taking a couple of extra days. A few hours with a Cajun woman and a little home brew can make any man forget his duties. You should go on back and tell your superiors to lighten up a little. Boy'll show back up when he sobers up."

Lacroix rested his hand suggestively on his gun belt. Just close enough to his sidearm to make a point, but not close enough to give offense.

"Is that an order?" Bolan asked.

"Nah, just a friendly suggestion."

"I think I'll hang around for a couple of days. After all, he may need a little assistance finding his way back home. Gentlemen."

Bolan blatantly turned his back on them and walked out the door.

After Bolan left, Smythe moved to the phone on the desk.

"What the hell was that?" Lacroix barked.

"It's not like I invited him, Duke," he replied. "He just

showed up here. I'm calling Mr. Costello right away. I can handle this."

"You're an idiot," Lacroix said. "He's here looking for Jack Rio. Did he tell you that? I haven't been informed about a formal investigation into his death, which means they're either keeping it below the radar or it's personal for this guy. I'd almost rather it was a covert operation. Personal matters can get messy."

"Yeah, that's who he's looking for," he said. "What of it? We can take care of him just like we did Rio."

Lacroix shook his head. "I don't know," he said quietly. "Something about that man sets me off. I wouldn't go underestimating him."

"You worry too much," Smythe said, picking up the phone.

"And you don't worry enough," the police chief said, moving to the door. "I'm going to look into this."

"You do that," Smythe said, dialing the phone number from memory. It rang several times before a smooth voice answered.

"Mr. Costello's residence," Victor Salerno said.

"Vic, it's Trenton."

"I've told you not to call me Vic, Smythe. Now what the hell do you want?" he asked. "Mr. Costello is busy."

"He's not too busy for this," he snapped. "Put him on."

"You've got a big mouth for a little man," Salerno replied. "Really big."

"Look, I just had a U.S. marshal in here looking for Rio, and he's not just going to walk away, so maybe you'd like to stop commenting on my big mouth and put the boss on."

There was a long silence, then Salerno said, "Hold on, little man."

There was the sound of muffled words, then, "Mr.

Smythe," Costello said as he came on the line. "I understand we have a small problem."

"I don't know how big the problem is," he said, then filled him in on his meeting with the U.S. marshal.

"And what did you tell him?" Costello asked.

"I told him to meet me at seven at Mosca's," Smythe said. In the background, he could hear the faint, painful moaning of someone—likely Jack Rio—being tortured.

"That will do nicely," Costello said. "I'll send along a welcoming committee and the problem will be solved. Good day, Mr. Smythe."

"Yes, sir," he said. "Thank you." He hung up the phone and sat down heavily. Things were going too far, too fast. Sooner or later, they'd all get caught and go to prison or worse.

And he agreed with Duke Lacroix. There was something about that man Cooper that gave him the willies. Smythe sat back down at his computer and went to his online banking. Maybe it was time to start thinking about moving some money.

3

In cities famous for their food, New Orleans stood out. But Mosca's wasn't just a well-known restaurant, it was a tradition meant to be celebrated, like Mardis Gras. At least that's what the waitress at the bistro told Bolan when he stopped in for a cup of coffee to go. While many restaurants were reputed for excellent food and service, only a few were esteemed for their ability to keep secrets. "If you want to talk about taking over the world, you go to Mosca's," she said, handing him his coffee.

While Bolan had no interest in taking over the world, a restaurant with that kind of reputation would certainly be online. He'd returned to his hotel room, locked the door and booted up his computer on the tiny desk that was as scarred as he was. Using a secure log-on, Bolan was able to find Mosca's website, several other mentions online, and, with a little clever manipulation learned from the Farm's computer genius Aaron Kurtzman, a back door into a set of FBI files on the Matranga Family itself.

According to the files, the Matrangas had been operating in New Orleans since at least the 1880s, but had virtually disappeared since the death of Carlos Marcello in 1993. Marcello had used Mosca's as the epicenter of his empire, having meets there for everything from personal meals to planning killings. Mosca's reputation of good food, incredibly discreet service and no questions asked had outlasted even the Mafia.

The location was far enough away from the hustle and bustle of New Orleans itself that it was possible to come and go without being seen by everyone. Bolan pulled up to the simple black-and-white building. It was fairly busy, and the parking lot was almost full. That suited him fine, and he parked on the far edge of the lot and rolled down his window. The smells coming from the restaurant were heavenly despite the heavy humidity in the air, and his stomach grumbled. He'd spent most of the afternoon reading the files he'd stolen from the FBI database and hadn't taken the time for lunch.

After watching for several minutes and seeing no signs of trouble, Bolan rolled up the window, got out of the car and locked it, then moved across the lot to the front door. He weaved his way through parked cars on the way there, as the lot didn't boast marked spaces, but was little more than a graveled area where people parked as they wanted.

He opened the door to a wave of smells and muted sounds. According to the file, Mosca's had renovated after Hurricane Katrina, and one of the improvements had been the installation of cork in the panels surrounding the booths, as well as the floors, to further dampen the noise. It had worked well, since while it was obvious that people were talking, it was almost impossible to discern single words.

There was an older man in a tuxedo shirt behind the bar, polishing glasses, and a middle-aged woman was standing near a podium. "Good evening, sir," she said. "Welcome to Mosca's."

"Thank you," Bolan said. "I'm meeting someone." He scanned the restaurant and spotted Smythe seated in a booth near the back. "There he is," he added.

"Oh," she said. "Mr. Smythe. He's expecting you."

"Thanks again," he said, turning away from her and crossing the restaurant, while keeping his eyes open for trouble. He didn't trust Smythe any further than he'd trust Lacroix. His suspicions about extensive corruption had been confirmed in the files he'd read, though nothing solid had been proved in recent years.

Smythe was seated with a beautiful woman, and both of them were drinking large glasses of red wine, presumably waiting for him to show up. They spoke together in low, heated whispers. Smythe finally spotted him and waved him over. The woman looked even more uncomfortable as she put her glass on the table. She really was striking, in a conservative cut, tan business suit, with a white blouse open at the neck and unbuttoned just enough to show a hint of cleavage.

Bolan reached the table. "Mr. Smythe, I don't recall your mentioning that you were bringing someone else along."

"I didn't, and she won't be staying long anyway," he said. "Marshal Cooper, this is my sister, Sandra Rousseau. Sandra, this is U.S. Marshal Cooper."

"Pleasure to meet you," she said, the words tumbling out of her mouth as she looked everywhere but at him. "I was just leaving." She tucked her purse under her arm and looked pointedly at her brother.

Bolan cleared his throat and her eyes met his. "I'm thinking that you may have a different definition of pleasure than I do. You look like a rabbit ready to dart."

"I…I apologize," she said, stammering. "It's been a long day for me. We had just ordered, but I really can't stay."

"You should eat something," Smythe said. "You'll feel better."

"There's no need to leave on my account," Bolan said. "Sit." It wasn't quite an order, but it was close.

She relaxed back into her seat. "I'll just finish my wine, then, and take my food to go."

Bolan sat down, ensuring that he had a good view of both the front door and the kitchen entrance. "Is there anything that you recommend on the menu?" he asked them.

"Oyster Mosca," Smythe said.

"I love their Italian crab salad," Sandra offered. She signaled a server who was passing by and asked for her order to be put in a container to go. Sandra looked anywhere but at Bolan. She fidgeted with her napkin and the pearl drop pendant on the chain around her neck.

Bolan considered their suggestions and discarded both. He ordered the Chicken à la Grande, and a glass of water. Sandra asked how he was enjoying New Orleans, and Bolan said that all he'd seen of it so far was his hotel and the DA's office.

"He's not here vacationing, Sandra," Smythe scolded. "He's on a case."

"Oh, I see," she said. "That's why you wanted to meet with Trenton, then."

"Yes," he said. "There's a missing U.S. marshal who was last known to be here in New Orleans. I'm trying to find him."

Bolan noted the hard glance that Smythe shot his sister, and she quickly changed the subject to places he might enjoy seeing, should he find the time.

"I was reading a little about the history of this place," Bolan said.

"Yes, interesting crime families and ruling the world," Sandra said.

"Something like that," Bolan said.

"The Matranga Family was very powerful in New Orleans for a long time. There was a rival Family that tried to come in at one point, the Provenzanos, but a battle waged in public brought that to an end and nearly ended the Matrangas as well."

"Sounds like you know your crime," Bolan said.

"I know my New Orleans history, Marshal Cooper."

"So what brought it all to an end?"

"A barrel murder."

"I've heard of a lot of ways to kill someone, but I've never heard of them being killed by a barrel," Bolan said.

"No not killed by, found in. They would kill someone, stuff them in a barrel and leave them on a corner for someone to find as a warning. The investigator that led the investigation into the cases was killed, and it was blamed on Italian immigrants. There were trials, lynch mobs and a lot of innocent people got killed, but Matranga escaped it all and reasserted himself."

Finally, the server brought her food in a container and served the other dishes. Sandra stood up to leave. Bolan stood as well.

"Thank you for the history lesson."

"Enjoy your stay, Marshal Cooper."

"Hold on," Smythe said. "I'll walk you out."

"Thank you, but I'm fine to get to my own car, I think. Besides, your food will get cold."

"It'll keep," he said, taking her arm firmly. "I insist."

"Smythe," Bolan said, "I'm about out of patience. Sit down and let's have our chat."

"I'll be right back," he said, already pushing his sister away from the table. "Have a glass of wine from our bottle. It's just the house merlot, but it's excellent."

Bolan watched as Smythe led the woman out through the front door. There was something cagey about the whole thing, but he wasn't interested in the sister. He wanted to know what Smythe knew. He ignored the wine on the table and asked for the server to refill his water, then turned his attention to the restaurant itself. He'd read that it had been renovated after the hurricane, but it looked like they'd been able to keep much of the original memorabilia intact. Ignoring the food despite his hunger, Bolan looked around the restaurant, scanning the many photos on the walls. The restaurant had the perfect mixture of old-world charm, polished wood and brass, and pictures from both Italy and New Orleans through the years.

Meeting at Mosca's with its known history was either a very bad joke or Smythe was a complete idiot. He had to have known that it had a loose connection to organized crime at one time, but perhaps he just liked the food. Still, if Rio had asked him about organized crime in New Orleans before he came down here, Bolan would likely have told him not to bother. But since his disappearance, the soldier was beginning to think that Rio's hunch had been far more accurate than even he'd originally anticipated. If Mosca's was involved, the FBI would surely know about it, so the pictures on the walls of the old notorious Mafia Family members were just that: pictures of infamous men.

Bolan glanced once more at the front of the restaurant and noticed that the bartender was no longer there, and neither was the hostess. The flow of customers had dried up, too. He walked over to the entrance and tried to look through the small window on the door, but there were only a few parking spaces directly in front of the building. Smythe was taking a long time, but something was clearly going on with his sister. Bolan returned to the table and sat down again.

Finally, after another five minutes had passed, he decided that Smythe was out of time. He got up and headed for the door, but wasn't even all of the way out, when he saw two large men standing next to his car on the far side of the lot. Smythe was nowhere to be seen, and Bolan made a mental note that the next time he saw him, bad things were going to happen to the little weasel. He moved across the parking lot cautiously, knowing they'd seen him come out, and simply tried to avoid being boxed in from behind.

As he reached his car, he saw that the two men were easily 250 pounds apiece. They wore pressed close-fitting khaki pants and dark T-shirts that revealed their muscles, and several tattoos. The bigger of the two looked like his biceps were going to pop through the material at any second. The other was slightly leaner and bald. Bolan stopped in front of the two men.

"Gentlemen, you're blocking my car."

"You're supposed to come with us," the bald man announced. "The boss would like to meet you."

Bolan laughed dryly. "And I'd like to meet him, but at a time of my own choosing. I think I'll pass for now, but tell him thanks for the invitation."

The Executioner had dealt with some "Family" members in the past. If they were the real deal, he knew he could have his hands full. He wasn't about to go with the two thugs, but it was important to use the false niceties anyway, then no one could claim offense later.

"You don't get it, mister. It wasn't really a request," Baldy said. He cracked his knuckles, trying to look menacing in a way that would have been intimidating to anyone who couldn't fight, but was almost comical to someone who could. "There are ways that we can be convincing," he added.

He nodded at his partner, and both men moved forward at the same time. Bolan stepped back, dropped low and leg-swept Baldy, which knocked him off balance and into the second man. The big guy stumbled back but kept his feet. The soldier didn't give him time to regain his balance completely, moving forward to plant a spin kick in the center of the other guy's chest.

He wanted them alive, since dead men didn't talk, so he

pressed on without weapons. Twisting, Bolan turned back and planted a solid right hook into Baldy's jaw, keeping him off balance and hurting. The big guy reached forward and grabbed Bolan's ankle. The Executioner went with it, dropped to his knee on the captured leg and did a low spin, connecting the back of his heel with the man's face. There was a crunching noise and a muffled scream as the guy's nose broke and blood flowed freely.

Both legs free again, the soldier stood up in time to catch a glimpse of Smythe moving away from his hiding place at a nearby vehicle. Bolan moved to go after him, but Baldy wasn't done yet, and hit Bolan from behind with a hammer shot to his back. Stumbling forward, he almost lost his balance in the loose gravel, but managed to catch himself and turn in time to block the follow-up swing.

As the man closed in, Bolan swung both hands wide and clapped him on the ears, trying to rupture his eardrums and forcing him completely off balance. A car peeled out of the lot, and he knew that Smythe was gone.

The second guy was getting slowly to his feet as Baldy staggered around holding his head. Bolan was tired of playing and pulled his Desert Eagle free. "Enough playtime," he said, pointing it at the man trying to get to his feet. "Don't move again, or your buddy is dead."

"Does it look like I'll miss him?" he snapped, still holding his aching head.

Disappointed that he wasn't deafened, Bolan shrugged and said, "No." He took two quick steps forward and buffaloed the guy on the ground, who went out like a light.

"You're dead," the bald thug said. "You know that?"

"I can see you're going to be difficult," Bolan replied, turning the gun in his direction. "But you'd be amazed how cooperative you'll become after I put a .44-caliber round in your leg."

4

From where he was on the table, Rio could see Nick Costello and Victor Salerno on the far side of the game room. A call had come through a few minutes ago that had made the big boss very unhappy. After hitting the end button on his cell phone, Nick stood quietly for a minute, rubbing the bridge of his nose.

Rio couldn't hear what was said between the two men, but both turned in his direction, and he knew that what he'd experienced so far was about to seem like a fond memory. He watched as Nick removed his coat. Forcing himself to grin, Rio said, "Everything okay? You look upset."

"Mr. Rio," Nick said, "I'm running out of patience with you. You will eventually tell me what I want to know about the U.S. Marshals Service border routines, but we're going to leave that for the moment and move on to a new subject."

"Cajun cuisine?" he asked brightly.

Salerno stepped into the punch that slammed into Rio's solar plexus, and the marshal felt his breath leave him in a rush. The room smelled of blood—his blood—and the cool, damp air of Costello's game room stank to high heaven, but he forced himself to draw another breath. He coughed, breathed again, then made himself start to laugh.

"Is that all you've got, you little bootlicker? My grand-mother hits harder than that."

Salerno growled and started to wind up again, but Nick raised a hand and stopped him.

"The problem, Mr. Rio, is that my associate here doesn't have the same level of imagination that I do. Sometimes, his heart just isn't in it. He prefers a good fight or a straight kill, while my approach is more subtle. I like to take my time and really get know what makes people tick. It truly enhances the experience."

Nick selected another blade from his implement tray. It was a double-edged, very thin tool that looked like some-thing an angry surgeon might use. He held it up to the light and turned it back and forth. "A good blade is a thing of beauty, yes?" he asked.

Before Rio could form a smart-ass answer, Nick stepped forward and slipped the knife into his knee, driving it behind his kneecap and twisting it. Rio couldn't help himself. He screamed in agony, and his vision filled with a reddish-brown haze.

Nick left the blade in place and waited for Rio to stop. When he did, the big boss said, "Now I think we can talk. Who is Marshal Cooper?"

He shook his head and his voice was weak as he said, "I don't know any Cooper." He could feel a thin trickle of blood running down his leg around the blade of the knife.

Nick placed a hand on the grip of the blade, not moving it, but the threat was there. "I don't believe you, Mr. Rio. Who is Marshal Cooper? Who sent him here?" He put a slight amount of pressure on the handle of the blade and Rio groaned.

"I don't know him!"

Salerno leaned in and slammed a fist down on his knee.

"The fuck you don't! Who did you tell that you were coming here? Someone knew you were here."

The pain was so excruciating that Rio thought he might black out.

"Enough, Victor," Nick snapped. Salerno backed away. Both men were obviously frustrated by something this guy Cooper had done.

"Marshal Rio," Nick said, "we're going to leave you for a while. I want you to think carefully until I return about what you'll say to me when I come back. If you don't answer my questions, then I'm going to..." His voice trailed off, and he shoved on the knife once more. Rio felt something give way in his knee, and he screamed again, knowing that he'd need surgery if he was ever going to walk again...if he lived.

"I'm going to make it hurt worse than this," Nick finished. "Come on, Victor."

"Why are we stopping, boss?" Salerno asked. "That Cooper fucked-up Tommy and Frank real good and left them in the trunk of their car!" He pointed at Rio. "And this guy knows something!"

"I believe he does, Victor," Nick said. "But we can deal with Cooper on our own, and given a little time, I think Marshal Rio will come around." He flicked the blade of the knife once more. "Besides, I'm leaving that there for him to think about."

Catching his breath, Rio said, "You think you can just kidnap a federal agent and people won't come looking for him? In another couple of days, this whole area will be covered with cops you haven't bought."

"Maybe," Nick said, leaning in to whisper his reply. "But by then both you and Cooper will be dead, and we'll be back in the shadows once more. So you want to think really hard about cooperating with me, Marshal." He reached forward and twisted the blade one more time. "Because you can die easy or hard, and it doesn't matter one bit to me."

Rio bit back the scream and whispered his hate between his teeth. The edge of oblivion wasn't far away. Rio wondered if there would be a time that it would overtake him and never let him come back.

"What's that you're saying?" Nick asked, leaning in a bit closer.

"Nick…"

"Yeah?"

Rio spit blood in his face. "Fuck you."

Nick pulled away and took out a handkerchief to wipe off his face. "You're a tough guy, all right, Marshall Rio. But even tough guys can be broken. I've seen tougher than you crying for their mommas." He turned to Salerno and gestured for the steps. "Let's go. When we come back, he either talks or you can feed him to the gators."

EARLY THE NEXT MORNING, Bolan found himself across the street from the DA's office once more. He sipped Turkish coffee and ignored the flirtatious waitress as he thought about what he'd learned the night before. The two thugs he'd taken care of outside Mosca's weren't willing to reveal much, but he'd gotten a name—Nick Costello—to go with the one he already had. Baldy had made it clear that Victor Salerno was the capo, but Costello was the big boss. He'd put both men in the trunk of their car as a message to Costello. By now, Salerno and Costello knew that Marshal Cooper meant business. Things were starting to heat up, but he wanted to deal with Smythe first.

People trying to kill him was part of the job, part of his life, and while it was about as personal as it could get, what really made Bolan angry was a man who wasn't willing to do his own dirty work. Smythe was spineless, and worse, he was on the take. Bolan wanted to make sure he paid for his crimes, so he'd camped out at the DA's office early, knowing Smythe would show eventually. There didn't really seem to be a quiet time on the streets of New Orleans, but after the morning commute things settled into a routine lull. Shortly after nine, he saw Smythe's car pull up and enter the parking garage, but the windows were darkened enough that Bolan couldn't see the interior.

The weather wasn't cooperating to be helpful, either. The oppressive humidity had turned into a light drizzle that made the surrounding morning gray more intense.

He waited until the car was gone from view, then crossed the street and slipped into the garage. Moving quickly, he reached the row where Smythe had parked and moved in. The car door started to open just as Bolan arrived, and he reached in and grabbed the man by the collar. A surprised shriek came from inside the car and Bolan let go. It wasn't Smythe, but his sister behind the wheel. He shoved forward, clapping a hand over her mouth before she could scream for help. Her eyes were wide and terrified.

"Look lady," Bolan whispered in her ear, "I haven't been in New Orleans long enough to get used to the humidity, and people are already trying to kill me or have me killed, including your brother." He shoved her backward and said, "Scoot over. You're going to tell me what you know or your brother's going to find you in the same condition that I left his goons in last night."

"What…but I don't know what you're talking about!" she said, as soon as he'd moved his hand away from her mouth.

"The hell you don't. Last night you were so itchy that you couldn't even manage to hold still through dinner. Then conveniently you and your brother disappear right before I'm attacked in the parking lot. And I saw him taking off from the parking lot, so excuse me if I think you're in this up to your eyeballs."

"But I'm here looking for my brother!" Sandra protested. "I left last night right after he escorted me to my car, but I didn't hear from him again and he never showed up at home." The concern in her voice did not move Bolan. He'd dealt with women in the past who could conjure tears on a moment's notice, and he suspected that Sandra had the acting abilities of any award show nominee.

"I can see you're really concerned for him. Did any of this concern happen to come my way when you were setting me up?"

"I didn't set you up," she said. "Look, I knew Trenton was up to something, but I had no idea what. I only met him there because he said that's where he was going to be."

"And you know nothing, right?" Bolan said, the skepticism clear in his voice. "Then I guess you're no use to me." He reached for the Desert Eagle under his jacket.

"Wait!" she said. "I didn't know anything about what he was doing last night, but I know other things that might help you. Trenton's…he's involved with the Mafia in some way. I don't know how exactly. But they've said they'd kill him if he didn't do what they said."

Finally we're getting somewhere, Bolan thought. "So what is it he does for them?"

"He makes sure that criminal cases against members of the Family don't get prosecuted," she said, hanging her head. "And they pay him. He can also make sure other cases are prosecuted or threatened to be prosecuted as leverage for the Family. His office fields a lot of the calls that would come from outside jurisdictions."

"So when is the real DA coming back?"

"He's supposedly been in D.C. for three months, but no

one has seen or heard from him or his family. My guess is they are either dead or in hiding."

"What did your brother tell you about last night?" he asked.

"Nothing! I swear!" she said. "Just that he was arranging a meeting of some kind. I stay out of everything. That's the only way you stay alive in New Orleans. Keep your head down and your mouth shut. You may not like me, Marshal Cooper, but sometimes you just do what it takes to stay alive. If that means you look the other way when your gut is gnawing at you, then you look the other way. I don't like it, but that's it." She tried to look away, but Bolan was not buying the tears or the distress. There was something about her that was still a little too cool and rehearsed.

"So why are you here?"

"Same as you, I guess—looking for my brother. Trying to save his life if he's gotten himself in a fix. I thought I would see if I could find something in his office that would help me. I love my brother and I don't want to see anything happen to him. There has to be some way I can help him."

"Well, why don't we go and look together?"

Bolan grabbed her arm and dragged her out of the car. Her foot slipped out of her heel as he was pulling her along, and he had to stop while she readjusted it. He was running out of patience and suspected that if he didn't find Rio soon he would be out of time. They moved to the elevator, got in and rode it to the fifth floor, where the DA's office was located. Before it opened, Bolan said, "Not a word or peep out of place while we're here," he said.

She nodded her agreement and followed him out of the elevator, then paused. "If you keep dragging me around, people are going to ask questions…or call the cops."

"Do you really think that makes me nervous?"

"If it doesn't, it should," she said. "They're all on the same side around here, in case you hadn't noticed, and I don't want to be on anyone's radar—especially not theirs. This isn't a safe town, not here or anywhere."

"Fine," he said, releasing her as they reached the entrance to the office. Bolan pushed her ahead of him, and she opened the door. They walked past Sally sitting at her desk in another low-cut dress, while she was desperately trying to hide the nail file and polish she was obviously using on her nails.

"Hey, Sally, my brother asked me to pick up a couple of things for him," Sandra said. "Do you mind?"

"Go ahead, hon, you know where everything is," Sally said, then added, "But you tell your brother to call the next time he's not going to be in the office. I was getting worried."

"Will do," she replied as they walked into the office. Bolan smiled and shut the door, then followed Sandra over to the desk, where he motioned for her to sit in the desk chair.

"Now," he said, "why don't you show me what it is you were so eager to find."

"I don't know what I thought I would find," she said. "I just thought I might find… I don't know, something that might tell me what's really going on with Trenton."

"Then you better start looking," Bolan said. "And hurry up."

5

After a pointless search of Smythe's office, Sandra came across a reference on an advisement memo to Chief Lacroix about a dockside warehouse that had been under investigation. According to the memo, Smythe had convinced the police that it wasn't worth looking into. As far as Bolan was concerned, that screamed it was worth looking into. He wrote down the address.

"Do you know how to get here?"

"Well, yeah," Sandra replied.

"Good, we're going."

"I don't want to go."

"Well, I don't want you to stay. So who do you think is going to win that argument?" Bolan asked.

Traffic between the DA's office and the docks wasn't heavy, but it was still slow-going since the streets were slicked with rain. It took almost an hour to wind through the French Quarter and find a place to park close to the warehouse. Bolan might have left Sandra behind, but he was convinced she knew more than she was letting on, so he'd insisted she come along. She was obviously unhappy about it, but Bolan didn't care. He intended on keeping her close until he figured out where Smythe had disappeared to, and more importantly, where this Nick Costello was hiding out.

They drove around the last curve, and Bolan pulled the car over into a parking space near a garbage Dumpster. He put it in park, cut the engine and looked over at Sandra.

"This is your last opportunity to tell me what is going on," he said. "If this is another setup or a trap of any kind, then I promise you that not only will I get out of it, but I'll hold you personally responsible for everything that's happened to me up to this point." He shifted in his seat and captured her gaze.

She fidgeted but didn't say anything.

"All right, let's go."

Bolan stepped out of the car and waited for Sandra to come and stand next to him. The area was quiet and they moved quickly down the side of the street. No one seemed to be watching them, and they reached the fenced area around the dock without incident.

The gate was open, and there was a small security shack with one guard. Bolan gestured for Sandra to remain quiet and waited for the guard to turn his back. Moving as swiftly and stealthily as a cat, Bolan got behind him, wrapped one strong arm around his throat and took him to the ground slowly, waiting until the man was unconscious. Then he stood up and gestured for Sandra to come closer. He moved the guard's jacket aside and showed her the small MAC-10 underneath. "Unless he's guarding Fort Knox, there's no way a regular warehouse security guard needs that," he said. "Come on."

They moved closer to the edge of the warehouse. The main entry door was locked, and Bolan looked at the security keypad.

"How do you propose to get in, Marshal?" Sandra whispered. "Got a Jedi mind trick to open it?"

Bolan ignored the gibe. "Just need a little bit of luck," he said, sliding a credit-card-sized object out of his wallet.

"What's that?" she asked.

"Magnetic scrambler," he said. "Almost all electronic locks have a magnetic component. This little toy sends a series of pulses that disable a magnetic lock."

"All electronic locks?"

"Not all of them," he said. "There are sophisticated locks that don't use magnetic codes, but anything like this, or hotel rooms, hospitals, even most airport initial access areas, this will work on. Saves time and beats having to call a locksmith on short notice." Bolan slid the card into place, then waited a moment for the lock system to register it. He tapped a small raised portion on the card, and the scrambler immediately popped the lock. The soldier opened the door and put the card back into his wallet.

"Come on," he said, slipping into the building and pulling his Desert Eagle free, as Sandra followed him into the dark warehouse.

Sandra looked down as they walked in, folded her arms across her chest and shivered from the change in temperature.

They main floor was almost completely filled with crates stacked end to end, and high enough to reach well above Bolan's head. Narrow walkways were left between the rows of crates, and he kept his back against the nearest stack, hoping for at least some protection in the event of an ambush. The warehouse wasn't well lit, but there was enough light to see the markings on the side of the containers. He stopped to look at the stamped markings. Picking one at random, he saw that it bore a FEMA insignia and a label that read Interior Plumbing, Copper Lines. The next one was PVC pipes. Bolan realized that the entire warehouse was filled with supplies sent to New Orleans after Hurricane Katrina to help the city rebuild—supplies that had been stolen and were likely being sold off or used in construction without cost.

Apparently, whoever was running the new crime family in New Orleans had decided that the hurricane was an opportunity to make money, without the risks of money laundering, drug smuggling or prostitution.

"FEMA," he said quietly to Sandra.

"So?" she asked. "After Katrina, the whole city was filled with construction supplies."

"Well, what the hell are they all doing here now?" Bolan asked.

"There are a lot of FEMA contractors. In case you hadn't noticed, there are still a lot of repairs that need to be done. What is it you think we're going to find here?"

"I think this is part of it," Bolan said. "Federal supplies shouldn't have come in this way, and they are usually utilized far faster than this. I think someone has been making money off hurricane reconstruction." He glared at her. "I don't suppose you know who has most of the reconstruction contracts in the city, do you?"

"Trenton told me it was Costello Construction," she said. "But this warehouse isn't in their name."

"No, it's not," Bolan said, remembering the painted lettering on the side of the building as they came in. "A subsidiary then."

"I could make a guess," she replied, "but you seem to like finding answers out all on your own. You don't trust anything I say, so why should I bother to try and answer any of your questions?"

"Look, Sandra, I'm not unreasonable, but I'm not stupid. I make my living by not getting killed, and I'm not about to start making mistakes now."

Bolan turned his attention to a set of crates behind Sandra. If he hadn't spent so much time in the Middle East, it likely wouldn't have jumped out at him, but he recognized the embossed stamping below the FEMA lettering on one of the crates. He moved forward, trying to remember the Hebrew he'd learned in the past and coming up short. Still the one word he did recognize was unmistakable—"rifle."

Bolan looked around and saw a forklift at the end of the aisle. He grabbed Sandra's hand and pulled her to it. She jerked her hand away.

"I'm getting real tired of you manhandling me. Where are we going now?"

"I need to see what's in that crate," he said, pointing to the one at the top of the stack.

"So go look, you don't need me in that contraption. What am I going to do, sit on your lap?"

Bolan looked at the one seat the forklift had and pointed at her.

"If you move, I *will* shoot you, no warning. Got it?"

She threw up her hands and backed up against a set of crates.

"I'll be standing right here. I'm as curious as you are."

Bolan climbed onto the forklift. He moved it into position and restacked the crates that had been hiding his target. He didn't bother with a crowbar to open the package. He was pretty sure he knew what was inside. He put the forklift in reverse and lowered the forks, shifted back into drive and drove the forks into the box, knocking it off the other side.

"Holy Jesus! Do you know anything about being inconspicuous?"

"I figure that since people are already trying to kill me, inconspicuous is really overrated."

Bolan cut the engine and jumped off of the forklift. They both ran around to the other side of the crates to see what prize he had freed.

The crate had smashed open when it hit the concrete floor, revealing a dozen or more Israeli assault rifles, Tavors from the look of them.

"Let me guess," Bolan asked her. "More reconstruction supplies?"

"Hardly," she said. "These have to belong to Victor Salerno. He works for Costello. I think we better get out of here. These aren't the kind of guys that you want mad at you."

"Salerno," he said. "Costello's enforcer? Got a brother named Tony?"

"I am," a voice said, echoing in the warehouse. "And I've got a brother named Tony."

"Seems he's gotten into a bit of trouble with the police," Bolan called out, shoving Sandra out of the way, even as gunfire erupted around them. He pulled out the Desert Eagle but held off firing, knowing that with all the flashes, finding a target took more patience. "Stay here and stay down," he snapped at her.

He moved quickly between the rows of crates. The warehouse was so packed that some rows were difficult to move through.

"Every warehouse has rats," Salerno called out. "You've just got to flush them out and kill them."

The Executioner kept his silence, knowing that to reply would give away his position. At the same time, because of Salerno's need for discourse, he knew that the man was above him, up near the offices. Bolan slipped around another stack of crates and waited.

"Lou, turn on the lights," Salerno said.

Bolan fired immediately, the Desert Eagle sounding like a cannon in the dark. The overhead fluorescents came on just in time for him to see Salerno topple over, yelling in pain. It hadn't been a kill shot, but a .44-caliber round in the shoulder was pretty attention getting all on its own.

"Your brother's dead, Victor," Bolan called. "Guess who's next?" He immediately changed position, running down a long, narrow row of crates.

Gunfire followed his steps, and he knew that the shooters were up on the catwalks above. He found a shadowed area and paused, looking for a path back to the door, where he'd seen the stairs going up to the catwalk when they came in.

"Marshal," Sandra whispered, coming up behind him.

Bolan spun and nearly put a round in her. "I told you to stay put," he said. "Did you think they wouldn't shoot you, too?"

She shook her head. "I swear this wasn't a setup," she said. "Follow me and we can get out of here."

"How do you know your way around here?"

"I've been here with Trenton before. He was looking at a FEMA contract and trying to get a mess straightened out. Really, we're not all as bad as you think."

"What makes you think I want to get out?" Bolan asked. "I want to get up there." He gestured overhead.

"Fine," she said. "The stairs are by the door anyway." She turned and started moving down one of the narrow rows.

Though he still doubted her, Bolan felt like his choices were limited. Letting Sandra go off by herself was probably the best choice, since he still thought she knew more than she was saying. On the other hand, following her was likely to end up with him getting killed. "Perfect," he said.

He turned to follow her, waiting for another round of gunfire. The silence was almost as bad, and he wondered how many men were up there. At least three or four more men judging by the shots fired. But Salerno was down, at least for the day, and maybe longer. Sandra turned down another row and Bolan followed, glancing back and behind, to make sure no one was sighting in.

In front of him, the row of crates widened into a open area. Sandra had come to a halt in midstride as several men came forward pointing their weapons. "Don't move," one of them said. He was an obese man who was sweating profusely.

Sandra turned to look back at Bolan, and the fat man said, "I mean it." She froze and he laughed.

Bolan took a few steps forward. "You don't need her," he said. "It's me you want."

"You're right," he replied. "I didn't mean you, you dumb broad. She's Victor's girl, so I'll let him decide what to do with her. It was you I meant."

Bolan shook his head disgustedly as Sandra turned and began backing away from him. "Is Vic okay?" she asked.

"He'll live," the man said. "Unlike your friend the marshal here."

Bolan didn't reply, just looked and waited for his opening. It was coming, and he tensed, waiting for the right moment to strike.

"I knew I should have left you behind," he said to Sandra. "You've been in it from the beginning. You know they probably still killed your brother, right?"

"I just help when Vic needs me," she said.

"And what about your brother?"

"My brother is none of your business."

He ignored her. "What's your story, tough guy?" Bolan asked the fat man. "Got a name?"

"Several, but none you'd have heard. I work for Victor."

Bolan sneered. "I can't call you late for dinner, that's obvious."

The man laughed. "You're funny, Cooper. A real comedian. You won't be laughing so much when Mr. Costello gets done with you. He likes to play with his new arrivals. Plus, I figure he's got to be tired of that other guy anyway."

"There's not much to laugh about where Mr. Costello is concerned," Bolan replied. "Killing is a serious business, and I plan to work extra hard to make sure he's bankrupt. You should watch how much fun you're having with the 'other guy,' it's likely to come back and bite you in the ass."

A soft step from behind was all the warning he received, and Bolan tried to turn, but he wasn't quite fast enough. The heavy rubber mallet slammed into the side of his head, and he saw stars as he went down. Standing over him was Salerno, blood still flowing from the graze on his shoulder. Bolan tried to lever himself back up, but couldn't manage to find his feet.

"You're done, tough guy," Salerno said, raising the mallet.

Dazed, Bolan raised a hand to block it, but never saw the fat man's booted foot as it smashed into his temple. The world went dark.

6

The Executioner woke to the hum of a mosquito swarm, the distant drone of an airboat, and the sure knowledge that he was in serious trouble. His head was pounding with every beat of his heart. His hands and feet were tied together, and he was strung up between two willow trees that were slowly bending with his weight. Blood dripped from the cut on his scalp into the water below, carrying his scent to the alligators that infested the area.

Trying not to move, Bolan scanned the water, looking for the telltale ripples that would indicate an approaching gator. Sure enough, he spotted several slowly closing in on him. For the moment, he was high enough from the ground that he would be safe, but eventually the trees would give way and he'd either be in the water or close enough that it wouldn't matter. Tied up as Bolan was, he couldn't even try to fight them off with a makeshift weapon.

Behind the veil of Spanish moss, the sound of the airboat grew closer, but Bolan didn't know if this was a friend or, more likely, another enemy, either set on killing him or just arriving to watch the gator show. One gator was becoming more curious. From the soldier's perspective the silhouette in the water looked about fourteen feet long. As the animal swam around the area that Bolan was hanging, a trickle of blood hit the water in front of it. The large jaws snapped out and slashed through the murky water. The tree limbs creaked under Bolan's weight and movement as he tried to inch his body away from the reptile. The big American's arms ached with the strain of his own weight.

The sound of the airboat was getting closer. He knew that his choices were diminishing with every second that ticked by. Using the little strength he had left, Bolan pulled on the limb that seemed most likely to break. The moist threads of the tree groaned in objection, but finally relented. The gator surfaced again, ready to take advantage of any situation. Bolan reached up and grabbed the sagging limb that still held his weight. It lowered inch by inch as he struggled to free his arm. The gator swam beneath him, the animal's tail flicking Bolan's boot on the way by as a subtle reminder that his time was almost up.

The airboat was almost deafening at this point. Bolan began to hope for the appearance of more of Costello's thugs—at least with them he knew how to fight and what he was up against. Carnivorous, prehistoric lizards were not really his area of expertise. Of course, fighting anyone was going to be difficult in his current situation. He strained harder at the branch, while watching the gators on final approach.

One of them circled and dived beneath the surface, and he wondered if the creature was going to come up beneath him, leaping out of the water to snatch him in its jaws, like he was a worm on a hook. Sure enough, his premonition proved accurate.

The gator exploded out of the water, jaws open, with an ominous hissing sound.

Bolan pulled hurriedly on the ropes, trying to lever himself higher into the air. The gator was practically standing on its tail, trying to reach him, when a heavy shot rocked the swamp air.

The gator slammed back down and into the water, still thrashing, but now in its death throes. Bolan twisted his head around and saw the airboat had rounded the veil of moss, and there was a huge black man standing in the bow, holding a rifle trained on the water.

A sense of relief swept through Bolan moments before the branches holding him up finally cracked, then snapped. Time slowed and Bolan had a half second to see a second gator heading his way as the water closed over his head.

The water wasn't particularly deep, and he pushed to his feet and shoved himself sideways as the gator attacked. Weaponless, he shifted in the water, prepared to go down fighting. The gator circled back and headed his way. Bolan braced for the worst just as he felt himself being lifted into the air.

Beside his ear, another shot rang out, this time from a .45-caliber MK23 that looked small in the hand gripping it. A deep, heavily accented voice said, "Don't struggle."

The second gator thrashed in its own death throes as Bolan relaxed until he finally felt the boat beneath his feet, then he caught his own weight and tried to find his balance. The Executioner was breathing heavily and dripping wet, but alive. He sat down and counted his own breaths for a minute, happy that they were still coming. He was a fighting man and to die that way would have been a terrible injustice.

"You had a close one there," the black man said, extending a hand to help Bolan to his feet.

He took the hand that was offered and levered himself upright. "I'd say thank you, but that hardly seems the word for your timely assistance."

"You're welcome," he said. Bolan was still struck by the

man's sheer size and deep voice. He was like a mountain that spoke.

"My name's Remy," he said, as though unaware of the effect he might have on people. "Normally, I keep myself to myself, but maybe you'd care to explain how you got yourself tied up between those trees."

"Matt Cooper," he said. "And it's a long story."

Bolan watched as the man moved back into the control chair and started the boat at a slow pace. He noted the Navy SEAL tattoo that the man was sporting below his cutoff sleeves. Remy saw him staring and looked back at him.

"You got a problem with the Navy?" he asked.

"No," Bolan said. "Just sizing up my situation."

"Then I'd say you don't have the high ground, if you know what I mean."

"True enough," he replied. "I'm a U.S. marshal, down here investigating a friend's disappearance. A fellow marshal."

"Ah, then you must be a friend of the marshal I hear tell about."

Bolan raised an eyebrow.

"Don't go fretting yourself," he said, guiding the boat around a large patch of trees hanging into the water. "I'm not involved with those thugs, but this swamp is small, and she talks if you listen. Everything that happens in the city shows up out here sooner or later. Rumors carry on the water, even in the swamp. Everyone tries to hide their secrets here, but I know them all."

The man spoke with a heavy Cajun accent, but Bolan easily understood him. "What is it you hear?"

"I hear a lot and I say very little. Costello has your boy, Rio, and he's got a finger in every pie in New Orleans. Word is that he's looking to expand outside the city," Remy said.

"And just a word to the wise," he added. "Everyone is involved, least everyone that matters. And those who aren't won't tell you nothin' because they don't want go visiting with your swamp friends back there."

Bolan tried to process what he was being told. So the only people who seemed to be on his side were an ex-Navy SEAL and Rio, who was either dead or incapacitated.

"Good to know," he said. "Is there more you can tell me about this Nick Costello?"

"He's a bad one," Remy said. "Word is old Italian Mafia Family type. His tough guy is Victor Salerno, but he's got the DA, the police chief and a good chunk of law enforcement all in his pocket. It's nothing new, but they figure if they have the court and the cops, plus all the bad guys on their side, they've got it all sewn up and nothing can stop them. So far they've been right."

"So what happened to Rio? They must feel invincible to kidnap a federal marshal."

"When your friend started poking around down here, he may just as well have hit a hornet's nest with a stick. Costello's people are into everything, and they weren't going to let one lone law dog stop them. Plus things have stayed quiet on the Fed side too long, which tells me they must have someone on the inside there, too."

Bolan thought about it for a minute and decided that if Rio wasn't dead yet, they had to want something from him. "You know anything else about Costello? You said the word was he was old Italy, but you don't sound convinced."

"I met him once," Remy said. "He was out in the swamp with some of his men. Just looking around, they said."

"They say what they were looking for?" he asked.

"No," he said, "but I don't think they were looking for anything. I think they were scouting the area. Costello bought an old mansion not far from here, paid a fortune to have it fixed up, and that's where he hides himself. Like a gator or a snake."

"Why don't you think he is what he says he is?" Bolan asked.

"I've been all over the world," Remy said. "Met a lot of folks and some just are who they say they are, but this guy... he isn't comfortable in his own skin, if you know what I mean. Don't doubt that he's bad *juju,* a real bad man, but he's not honest about who he is or what he wants, even to those who are in the swamp with him. That tells me a lot about the man right there. I grew up in this area, met some of the old Family types."

Bolan sat back and pondered. If Costello wasn't really who he claimed to be, then there could more trouble from within his own circles than there was from law enforcement. Nothing fit together quite right.

Remy guided the airboat to a slow halt, and it coasted up to a small island of land. "So, you want to tell me again how you're a U.S. marshal, 'cause I'm not believing that for a minute."

"Why do you say that?"

"'Cause down here a marshal is gonna end up dead or eaten by a gator," Remy said. "And I do believe you might have given that gator a good fight. I don't hold much with secrets, but I understand some that have to be kept."

"I'm here to help Jack Rio," Bolan said. "Does the rest of it really matter?"

Remy chuckled and shook his head. "No, sir," he said. "Not one little bit." He climbed out of the seat and moved to the front of the boat. "Come on, then." Remy jumped to the ground and tied the airboat to a very concealed post. "You're going to need something more lethal than that leech sucking on your arm if you're going to help your friend."

Bolan looked down at the black sluglike creature attached to his skin. He reached down, then carefully pried it off. "Who are you?" he asked, following him onto land.

"I ain't nobody," Remy said. "I served my country, and when that was over, I came back here."

"To live in the swamp?" Bolan asked.

"To live in peace," Remy said. "Follow me. My place is up this way."

Bolan followed the man deeper into the heavy trees, and was surprised to discover a well-built cabin hidden behind the veils of moss. "A good spot to disappear to," Bolan noted. "It'd be almost impossible to find unless you knew what you were looking for."

"That was the idea," Remy said. "And I'd bet my boots that if you left here, you couldn't find it again." He led the way to the door, opened it and went inside, gesturing for Bolan to follow along.

Inside was snug and comfortable. There was only one large room, with a small table and kitchen dominating one side, and a bed and recliner on the other. "There's an out-house in the back if you need to use the facilities," Remy said, moving to a large trunk at the foot of the bed. He opened it and began digging through it until he came up with a pair of sweatpants and a T-shirt. He tossed them to Bolan.

"Put these on," he said, "until your own dry out."

Bolan changed out of his own soggy clothing, removing several leeches in the process. "They're fast," he said, peeling off another one. "I wasn't in the water for that long."

"They're everywhere," Remy said. "Probably picked 'em up when Costello's men were dragging you out here." He took Bolan's clothing outside and secured it to a line, then returned.

Bolan sat down at the small table, accepted the offer of a beverage and a sandwich from the man, then asked him about Costello's activities.

Remy shrugged. "I don't know much for certain, but I can

make some guesses. Drug running for sure, lots of that out here because it's easy to hide. It's odd though."

"What's that?" Bolan asked.

"Costello hiding away out here. Don't those Mafia fellows prefer to live in the city?"

"That's been my experience," he replied. "Closer to their interests. Can't shake someone down for money if there are no warm bodies."

After they finished, Remy moved to the bed once again, but this time, he lifted it, revealing a trapdoor beneath. Opening it, he began removing various weapons for Bolan's inspection. "Pick out something that works for you," he said, "then I'll take you to Costello's compound."

Thanking him, and regretting the loss of his Desert Eagle, Bolan picked out a combat knife, as well as an H&K .45, with an extra magazine. "These will do until I can get back to my own gear, but I need to do that before facing Costello. It's time for me to check in with some people and get some better information than I've gotten right now."

"I can get you back to the city," Remy replied. "Unseen."

"Good," Bolan said. He went outside and returned with his own, still damp, clothing. After inspecting it for leeches, he dressed, then armed himself. "Better," he told Remy.

"Then let's get on our way," he said. "The sooner you get Costello out of my swamp, the happier I'm gonna be."

"He bothers you?" Bolan asked.

"Nah," Remy said, "but gators don't either, and I kill plenty of those, too."

7

There were two unmarked police cars parked outside his hotel, but no sign of the officers themselves in the lobby. While there was no guarantee they were interested in him, or even in his hotel, Bolan had a feeling that something was amiss. He carefully scanned the lobby as he passed through it, noted the clerk's overt indifference, then moved to the stairs. He was on the top floor, the eighth, and it was a long hike up the stairs.

Bolan lunged up the last of the steps to his floor. He opened the door and peered into the hallway, which was clear, then moved quickly to his room. Remy's help had been invaluable, but he needed to resupply and get in touch with Stony Man Farm. There was going to be a reckoning down here.

The door to his room was slightly ajar when he reached it, and he paused. The gun he had would be too loud if trouble ensued, but his Navy SEAL Combat Knife would be silent and nearly as effective, especially in the close quarters of a small hotel room. He reached for the blade with his right hand as he slid his left along the cracked door and pushed it quietly open. Inside, he saw three figures, one of whom he recognized on sight. Chief of Police Duke Lacroix leaned against the battered dresser.

Lacroix's senses were well-honed as he looked up to see Bolan standing in the doorway.

"What the hell are you doing here? What's this all about?" Bolan demanded.

"Marshal Cooper," Lacroix said. "I'm glad you could join us. We've got some questions for you." The two other men, detectives by the look of them, stopped searching and moved toward the doorway.

"Not until I see a warrant and you tell me what's going on here," he said.

Lacroix pulled a folded sheet of paper out of his suit coat and snapped it open, then handed it to Bolan, who scanned the contents quickly. The warrant authorized a search of his hotel room and included a custody order. He was to be questioned in regards to the death of Trenton Smythe.

A cold feeling flooded his being. When cops or DAs died, everyone in law enforcement took it personally—and with good reason. Most of the men and women who served were upstanding citizens, trying to make the world a better place. Smythe had been an exception to that, but Bolan wasn't sure he deserved death, either.

"What happened to Smythe?" he asked, handing the warrant back.

"You tell me, Marshal," Lacroix said. "He was found dead in your rental car."

Resisting the urge to swear, Bolan gritted his teeth. "Cause of death?" he asked, knowing the answer.

"Gunshot wound to the head," he replied. "Care to guess what the coroner thinks about the caliber?"

"I'm going to say a .45," he said. "Standard issue for U.S. marshals."

"Is that a confession?" Lacroix asked. "It'd make my job a lot easier."

"Hardly," Bolan said. "Just a guess based on the corruption I've seen in your fair city so far."

"A pretty good guess," he said. "I don't think it was a guess, though. I think you knew because *you* pulled the trigger." He jabbed a finger in Bolan's direction. "And as far as corruption goes, are you saying Smythe was dirty?"

Bolan laughed. "Dirty?" he asked. "He was so filthy he was mud, and you know it."

"What are you saying, Marshal? You accusing me of something?"

Bolan waved Lacroix over to the side of the room, and when the two detectives started to follow, Lacroix motioned them to stay back.

Lowering his voice, Bolan said, "I don't know how deep into this mire you are, Chief Lacroix, but you might want to reconsider your position here." He allowed his eyes to bore into the other man. "Here's what going to happen in this city, *Chief.* I'm going to take down every last son of a bitch involved in Costello's operation and my fellow marshal's disappearance. I'm going to take them down hard, and they're going to pay. This might be your one and only chance to get out of this with your skin intact."

Lacroix appeared to consider the Executioner's words for a moment, then began to laugh. "Who the hell do you think you are, Marshal Cooper?" The chief stepped forward, placing a meaty hand on Bolan's shoulder. "*Here's* what's going to happen. I'm going to place you under arrest, and me and my boys are going to question you right here in the privacy of this hotel room. And when we're done questioning you, we'll take you by the hospital to get patched up before we toss your ass into jail where you'll rot until trial, or until someone decides that wasting time on you really isn't worth it and just takes care of the problem."

"So, I take it your answer is no?" Bolan asked.

"My answer is that you're going to be arrested now. I'm going to get all of the information I need, and then I'll take you in and a judge can decide what to do with you," Lacroix said, reaching for his cuffs.

"I don't think so," Bolan said, grabbing Lacroix's left arm, then twisting it and using the leverage to slam him into the wall. He heard the detectives coming and didn't hesitate or slow his movements, but spun, pulling the combat knife free and ducking under the rush of the closer man. Bolan sliced backward, taking out the detective's hamstring. The man uttered a high, wailing cry as his leg crumpled beneath him.

The second detective lunged forward, and Bolan moved inside the man's upraised arms and headbutted him, snapping the bridge of his nose like a twig. The detective stepped back, stunned, shaking his head. When he noticed his blood pouring from his nose, he howled with rage and slammed into Bolan full force, knocking him backward into the dresser. The soldier shoved him away hard, then snapped a front kick into his sternum, knocking the detective across the room.

Lacroix had gained his feet, and now reached out to grab Bolan, but the Executioner reversed his momentum, pinning the police chief's arm at the top, turning sideways, then driving his right elbow into Lacroix's ribs. The air went out of the overweight man like a popped bicycle tire. Bolan followed up with a sharp right to the guy's face, and Lacroix went down once more.

While the detective with the slashed hamstring rolled on the floor, the other man attacked Bolan again. He didn't want to kill these men. While he had suspicions about Lacroix, he didn't know for sure how dirty he or the detectives really were. To kill them out of hand wasn't part of how he saw his role in the world. Bolan took the detective down one more time, using a sharp kick to the knee, followed with an elbow strike to the cheek, and the man landed on top of Lacroix, who was screaming for him to get up.

Seeing his only opportunity, Bolan grabbed his duffel bag off the bed and hightailed it out the window and on to the rickety fire escape. The entire structure felt as if it could come down around him at any second, but he was halfway to the ground before he heard the shouting of Lacroix and the still mobile detective following him.

"Go get him, you idiot!" the police chief yelled. Bolan heard as much as felt the fire escape adjust to the extra weight on it, and was glad to be close to the ground.

He reached the end of the fire escape, jumped the last six or so feet and headed down the alley. At the first inter-section, he went left and simply kept twisting and turning, avoiding refuse and several sleeping homeless men before he stopped to rest. Crouching near a garbage Dumpster near the mouth of an alley, he watched the alley behind him for several minutes before he was convinced that he'd lost his pursuers. Satisfied, he opened the duffel bag and saw that everything was still inside.

The biggest item—a smaller, silver briefcase—was what he truly needed. He pressed his thumbs against the locks and let the microchips read his prints, which opened the case. Inside was a global cell phone, an envelope with several hundred dollars in cash, as well as the paperwork for an alternate ID and a Micro Desert Eagle. Like the Walther PPK, it was perfect to stick in your pocket as a carry-concealed weapon. While the .380 round didn't have the same exciting impact as his usual .44-caliber rounds, it would do as a backup gun. One thing an experienced shooter learned was that being comfortable with a particular weapon or even brand, was almost as important as consistent practice. He put the weapon away, then pulled out the phone.

He dialed a number from memory, hit the send button and

waited to be connected. Eventually he heard the reassuring voice of Hal Brognola, director of the Sensitive Operations Group, based at Stony Man Farm, and the man who ran the show.

"Striker," Brognola said.

"I'm glad I reached you, Hal," he said. "I'm in it up to my eyeballs here in New Orleans."

"What kind of trouble do you have? Do you have any leads on Rio?"

Bolan quickly sketched in what he knew, then added, "Hal, Rio wasn't just onto something random down here, he was onto something huge. The Mafia is alive and well in the Big Easy, and the corruption is top to bottom."

"The authorities should have listened to the marshal when he started having suspicions. Do you think he's still alive?" Brognola asked.

"I don't know," Bolan said. "Maybe. If so, they must want something from him, but I can't figure out what it would be."

Brognola was quiet for a moment, then sighed. "I can't think what it would be, either, but then we don't know everything this Costello has a finger in. I'll look into some of the cases he's been involved with and see if I can dig up anything. Are the locals any help at all?"

"Plenty," Bolan said, "if you mean trying to pin a murder rap on me and stringing me up as gator bait, then yeah, very helpful. At the very least, the chief of police and the DA's office are both dirty. They just tried to arrest me for the murder of the assistant DA."

"You aren't normally quite so sarcastic," Brognola said. "They must have really pissed you off."

"I'm not happy," Bolan admitted.

"Who was the assistant DA?"

"A man named Trenton Smythe. He and his sister are

involved, but it sounds like Smythe is dead. The DA himself is MIA—can you look into his story as well? If he's not dead, then he's hiding somewhere."

"Yeah, I'll check it out. So maybe we should get you out of there," he said. "We'll send in a recon team and take them out. I know you don't like giving in, but these are not great odds."

"That's not going to happen, Hal. No one leaves me for alligator bait without getting a personal visit in return. And I'm not just going to leave Marshal Rio here. I'm in it until it's over."

"All right, then," he said. "I'll work on what I can from my end, try and track your missing DA and see what I can dig up on these other guys. What else do you need?"

Bolan thought about it for a minute, then said, "I need a full refit of field gear, including a Desert Eagle, communication units, the whole kit." He paused, then added, "And a local law-enforcement contact who isn't dirty. There has to be someone down here who isn't crooked."

Bolan could hear the sound of keys clicking, then Brognola said, "There's an FBI agent down there named Grady Black. He's done some back-channel work for us, and he's clean. I'll arrange for him to meet you with supplies and offer any help he can."

"When and where should I meet Black?" Bolan asked.

The keys tapped once more. "Your phone is equipped with GPS," he said. "I'm sending the coordinates now. It's an old, abandoned farmhouse in Belle Chasse. Pretty remote. Can you make it out that far?"

"I'll get there," he said.

"All right. I'll have Grady Black meet you there in about two hours. And Striker…" Brognola's voice trailed off.

"Yeah?" he said.

"Try to get Rio out of there alive, and keep the body count

down. New Orleans is still a hot button issue for the Feds. We can send a bunch of guys in, but no one is going to like it, and it would be as messy as hell when I had to explain it to the Man."

"I'll do my best," he said, ending the call. Bolan put the briefcase away in his duffel bag, and decided it was safe to keep the cell phone for the time being. Once he had been re-supplied, he'd ditch it and get a new one if he needed to. He knew that Costello's people would be monitoring the channels and didn't want to make tracking him any easier than it had to be.

Bolan stepped onto the street and began walking, looking carefully but casually into the windows of the parked vehicles. He rubbed his head as he walked, running his fingers over the healing cut from the rubber mallet. Eventually he found what he needed: a car with the keys in it. The old Malibu wouldn't win any beauty prizes in its current condition, but it had an engine that would make any young man weep.

He climbed in, started the engine and drove off, heading for Belle Chasse and the beginning of the end for Nick Costello and his entire operation.

8

The farmhouse in Belle Chasse was close to the naval air station, though Bolan would've been hard-pressed to determine what could have ever been farmed there. It seemed like it was too close to the water to have been much good for anything. The house was pretty run-down, with rotted clapboard siding, and clearly deserted. Strangle weeds had grown up in the gravel driveway, most of the windows were broken out and some kind of snake was curled up on the wooden doorstep taking in the sun.

Bolan parked the stolen car behind a large grouping of lilac bushes and went to the back of the house. The door there had long since fallen in, but due to its angle, he couldn't see inside.

The soldier pulled the Micro Desert Eagle from his pocket and moved along the back of the house, then slipped inside. The old floor creaked with protest as he placed his foot on the wooden slats, and for a moment, he wondered if he was going to fall through.

"Black?" he called.

"Cooper?" a voice answered from the next room.

"That's me," he replied.

Grady Black moved out from the next room and holstered his weapon. He wore the traditional FBI suit of black and white, and a pair of Ray-Ban sunglasses were stuck in his suit coat pocket. Bolan saw that Black was younger than he expected, perhaps early thirties, with dark brown hair, pale skin and nervous blue eyes. The soldier also noticed that he moved with a kind of grace.

Black gave him a critical once-over, then said, "You look like you've been run over by a truck."

"I only made it out of the city by the skin of my teeth," Bolan said. "I ran into a rough crowd."

"This is a bad place, all right. New Orleans will eat you alive," he said. "It was bad down here ten years ago, and it's just gotten worse since Katrina. The biggest problem is corruption, and those who aren't corruptible have a real bad habit of dying mysteriously. It's made it difficult to nail the bastards involved, because we can't put a finger on them."

"It's hard to put your finger in the leak when you're standing in the flood," Bolan said.

"So I've been hearing," he said. "Brognola brought me up to speed on your situation. I hear you've been making friends all over the city. Especially with Nick Costello."

"You've got something on him?"

"Everything I've got, I brought to you here," Black replied. "Along with the supplies you requested."

Bolan followed him into the kitchen, noting the careful grace the agent displayed as he moved around floorboards that had rotted out or looked weak. The dark room that had once been the center of a family's life sat empty and lifeless. The sinks were gone, with only broken pipes sticking out of the floor, and most of the cabinet doors had come off. An old laminated table and two metal chairs were the only furnishings remaining, and these had obviously seen better days.

On the table was a large black briefcase. Black walked over to it and popped the latches, opening it completely. Bolan moved to stand next to him as he removed a file. He saw the matched set of Desert Eagles and removed them without hesitation. He checked the magazine on each one, and when he was satisfied, he nodded to Black.

"You know," the agent said, "those are very big guns. It's like carrying a cannon. You ever think about using something different?"

"Yeah," he said with a hint of humor, "once in a while, I think about carrying a cannon."

"Fair enough," he said. Black held up the file. "Here's what we know about Costello. Back in the mid-nineties, Nick Costello was arrested several times on drug charges, but they never stuck—everything was either dropped or expunged. Then he fell off the radar until right after Hurricane Katrina. Suddenly he was in New Orleans running a construction company and making money off the Feds hand over fist. We know he's dirty, we know he's Family, but everything we've got is circumstantial. His damn lawyer would have him out in less than a day." Black handed over the file. "I just don't have enough to put all the pieces together and really nail him."

Bolan opened the folder and glanced at its contents. "What about Lacroix? How's he linked to Costello?"

"We know he's very wealthy for a chief of police," Black said. "He was pretty good at hiding the money until recently, but we can't prove where it's coming from. Until we have that, picking him up would be pointless, too." He paused, then added, "Oh, and get this. When Costello showed up in New Orleans, he was in debt up to his eyeballs. Then, all that debt suddenly disappeared right about the time he starts working the town hard. If we're really lucky, we not only get Lacroix connected to Costello, but we get whoever is backing Costello, as well."

"What do you need?" Bolan asked.

"Records would be nice," Black said. "A confession would even be better."

Bolan nodded. "Everything else I asked for in the vehicle?"

"Yes," he said. "It's a black Ford Expedition, parked another quarter mile down the road on the right. There are a lot of vehicles there—it's a good fishing spot."

"Good," he said. "Take the vehicle I brought back into the city for me?"

"Is it stolen?" Black asked.

"Borrowed," he corrected. "See how I'm asking you to return it for me?"

Grady sighed heavily. "Do you think you can get what I need to make this bust, Cooper?"

"Leave it to me," he said. They shook hands and Bolan slipped back out of the house and jogged down the road to get the SUV and head back into the city. There was plenty of work left to be done, and he still needed to rescue Marshal Jack Rio.

BOLAN SPOTTED one of the unmarked police cars from outside his hotel parked several blocks away, outside a diner. He parked the SUV around the block and finished outfitting himself with clean clothing. He put one of the Desert Eagles in a shoulder holster beneath a light windbreaker, and left the other one in a concealed compartment in the back. The Micro Desert Eagle went in a lower back holster and the combat knife into his boot. Bolan still carried the global cell phone and felt more like himself than he had in hours. New Orleans seemed to have the effect of making people feel out of place.

He locked the SUV and made sure the theft deterrent was engaged. It wouldn't stop a determined thief, but the vaguely smart ones would skip it for easier prey. Then he jogged around the corner and back up the street to where the cop car had been parked. He was playing a hunch, but as he walked by the plate-glass window, the Executioner saw that his instincts were good.

Duke Lacroix was just sitting down to dinner, a prospect he obviously enjoyed. Using a small pair of field glasses that adjusted for the tempered glass, Bolan watched as he cleaned his plate in the diner, then sat back to loosen his belt. This wasn't a man who let a little thing like killing innocent people or breaking the laws he was supposed to enforce ruin his appetite.

Bolan waited patiently for the chief to exit the diner. As Lacroix walked to his police car and unlocked the door, the Executioner moved out of concealment and behind the police chief. Barely slowing, he grabbed him by the back of the head and knocked it hard against the door frame. Staggering, Lacroix slumped forward.

The soldier opened the back door, shoved Lacroix in, then shut it behind him. He noted a woman watching the action from the sidewalk and he gave her a small smile. "Too much wine at dinner," he said. "Can't hold his liquor."

She laughed and continued on her way.

Bolan drove the car out of town, and as they reached the outskirts, Lacroix stirred in the backseat. He moaned like a man with a very bad headache before rousing himself enough to sit up and look through the bulletproof glass guard that separated the backseat from the front.

"What the fuck do you think you're doing?" Lacroix snarled.

Bolan looked at him in the mirror, then signaled for a turn before answering. "I made some friends out here the other day. Since you promised them a good meal and they got stiffed, I thought you might like to have a visit with them. Maybe even find some way to make it up to them."

"I don't know what you're talking about, Cooper, but if you don't let me go, you won't live to regret it." Lacroix slammed his fist into the divider and cursed.

Bolan made the turn, then took another side road that quickly became a rutted dirt path. "I'm thinking that your focus should be on whether or not *you're* going to live, Lacroix. You worry too much about me, and you could get distracted at a critical time."

The path took them behind the trees and into the swamp itself. Bolan pulled the car to a stop when it was clear he couldn't go any farther without risking getting stuck. As it was, the tires were coated in a muddy slime. He turned in his seat and looked at Lacroix.

"I'm going to give you one chance, Lacroix, to tell me everything—who killed Smythe, your connection to Costello, all of it."

Lacroix stared at him through the divider. "I'm not telling you shit, Marshal. You can threaten whatever you want, but you and I both know that you'll never convict me getting a confession like this, so go to hell."

The soldier stepped out of the car, jerked the back door open and grabbed Lacroix by the back of his shirt as the chief tried to make a run for it. Bolan shifted his weight slightly and landed a clean punch to the solar plexus. Lacroix's breath rushed out of him in one long whoosh and he leaned back against the car, staring up at the Executioner with genuine hatred in his eyes. Which meant he wasn't really afraid yet, and Bolan knew he'd have to rectify that immediately.

He stepped in close. "You've got me all wrong, Lacroix. You see, I'm not really a U.S. marshal, and I don't really give a damn whether any of this ever goes to a court of law or sees the light of day. I care about justice, and I care about my friend Marshal Rio." He slammed another punch into the man's abdomen. "And believe me when I say that justice is going to be served here, but it's going to be done my way."

All the blood had drained from Lacroix's face, and he was looking at Bolan out of the corner of his eye, obviously trying to determine if he was serious and telling the truth. Bolan needed Lacroix to talk, and if that required more convincing he was happy to oblige the man. He drew the combat knife from his boot and slid the blade up to Lacroix's carotid artery.

"Now," he said, his voice dropping into a low, quiet register that promised violence and pain. "Who killed Smythe? Was it you or Costello?"

"You killed Smythe!" Lacroix said. "Remember?"

His patience was wearing thin. Bolan yanked Lacroix away from the car and pushed him a couple of steps into the muddy water. The man's dress shoes squelched in the mud, but he froze like a spotlighted jackrabbit when the blade sliced a thin cut along his jawline.

"Facial wounds bleed a lot," Bolan whispered. "Almost as much as a head or scalp wound." Blood dripped into the water. "But I'm thinking that even that little bit will be enough to draw every gator for ten miles around."

Lacroix began to breathe faster, and sweat soaked his skin and face. He looked across the bank at the gators that had been napping and sunning themselves. One began to get curious about the visitors and slipped into the water, beginning his patrol.

"See there?" Bolan asked, gesturing. "We'll have company in no time."

"All right, fine," Lacroix snapped. "I help Costello from time to time, but just trying to get things to his warehouse."

"I think you're a lying bastard," Bolan said, and with a kick he took out Lacroix's knee from under him. The man splashed into the water, then got to his knees, but froze when he felt the blade touch his face once more. The cut had opened wider in the short struggle and blood was dripping freely, while Lacroix's face was about six inches from the water.

"Okay, okay!" he said. "I killed Smythe. He was a problem and wouldn't keep his mouth shut."

"Where's the proof?" Bolan asked.

Lacroix sagged as the confession ran out of him. "The body was moved in my car first. You can check it out yourself."

"Tell me about Costello," Bolan said. "What's his game?"

"He moves stuff," he said.

"Like what?"

"I don't know, drugs maybe."

Bolan pushed the chief's head all the way into the murky water, then pulled him back up, sputtering.

"You know more than that," he said. "Guess it's scalping time. Those bleed like a sieve."

"Guns! Guns!" Lacroix screeched. "He moves guns."

Bolan stepped back and dragged the man onto shore where he collapsed, then turned to the trees. "You get all that Agent Black?"

Black stepped out from his cover and put cuffs on Lacroix. "I got every word," the FBI agent said. "It's a good start."

"It's not enough," Bolan said. "How long can you keep this quiet?"

"Why?" Black asked. "Let's just arrest these guys."

"If we move in now, then we lose Costello, and Rio will be dead for sure. Give me twenty-four hours."

Black shook his head. "I can give you twelve, but twenty-four is probably too long. I can try, but people are going to notice that the chief of police is missing."

Bolan thought about it for a minute, then said, "Have someone call in on his behalf. Tell his office that he's helping in a federal investigation and will check in as soon as he can."

"That might buy us some time," Black said. "I still don't think we'll get twenty-four out of it, though."

"Neither do I," Bolan said. "But it will make some of the people likely to hear it very, very nervous."

The agent caught on and smiled at the man. "I like the way you think," he said.

"Me, too," Bolan replied, then looked down at his watch. "I've got to keep moving. You can handle this from here?" He nudged Lacroix with the toe of his boot.

"Just like any other sack of trash," he said. "Except I'm bringing it in instead of taking it out."

9

The news wasn't good, and the longer Nick Costello listened to his informant over the phone, the angrier he became. Across the room, Victor Salerno's face was impassive. Pushed to his limit, Nick said, "Just find the son of a bitch, you idiot! Find him and bring him in! You're a cop, for God's sake."

Then he turned and threw his cell phone across the room with all his strength. It shattered on the wall, littering the tile floor with sharp shards of plastic. The detectives who had attempted to take Marshal Cooper into custody with Lacroix had reported back the failed attempt and then idiotically left the chief unprotected. Several hours later, Lacroix was apparently in FBI custody, arrested by an agent Nick had never heard of. Of course, the official story was that he was assisting in an investigation, but Nick had contacts at the FBI office in the city and he already knew that Lacroix was being grilled and would likely be charged.

He lit another cigarette from the nearly depleted pack and paced back and forth, leaving a trail of smoke as he went. This entire situation seemed outrageous to Nick. How could one man cause so much trouble? He took another drag from the cigarette, then crushed it out in an ashtray on the counter. He turned to Salerno.

"We've got to get this situation under control immediately. I've got a feeling that things are spinning out of control, and I don't like it. Rio needs to talk, and he needs to talk now. If we can't get those weapons moved, we're well and truly fucked."

"So let's make him talk," Salerno said. "And stop screwing around with it."

They moved quickly through the main house and back down to the game room. Rio remained chained to the table, the handle of the knife still sticking out from his knee. He saw them enter the room and turned his head away. Exhaustion marked his face.

Nick stared at him for a moment and felt all his earlier rage return, and then it boiled over into an angry scream.

"You're going to talk this time, tough guy," he said when he calmed slightly. "You're going to tell me everything or the Devil can take you."

AFTER HE LEFT Black, Bolan returned to the city and picked up his vehicle once more. With Smythe dead, his next best source of information was Sandra. But he didn't have the first clue as to where she might be. After giving it some thought, he looked up the address for the city morgue on the built-in GPS in the SUV. Smythe's body was most likely there, awaiting a full autopsy, and if Sandra had been notified, he might find her there. Considering how his luck had run so far in this city, he didn't hold out much hope, but it was the best shot he had at the moment.

Bolan parked the SUV and crossed the busy street. The main city morgue was a brown nondescript facility. As he entered the main doors, he noted that it was also a busy place, with plenty of civilians waiting to begin dealing with the machinery of death. The staff looked overworked and overwhelmed, and Bolan guessed that there was still plenty of

Katrina aftermath they were dealing with. He moved down a narrow hallway where people sat and waited to identify bodies. Not seeing Sandra there, he turned the corner and nearly ran into her coming back from an office down the hall. Her head was lowered, and she looked pale and ill. She didn't notice Bolan until he was right in front of her.

"Pardon me," she started to say, then looked up, her eyes widening.

"Hello, Sandra," Bolan said, moving in close enough for the threat in his voice to be clear. "We need to have a talk, don't you think?"

She started to turn, and Bolan easily caught her by the arm. He didn't like using violence or even the threat of violence with women, but whatever game this woman had been involved in had resulted in two attempts on his life, and he was running out of time and patience. Whatever she knew, she was going to talk.

She struggled briefly in his grasp, still trying to run, and Bolan spun her around and up against the wall with enough force to stop her struggles. "I've killed people for less than what you've done to me," he said.

"Go ahead," Sandra said, her eyes filling with unshed tears. "What does it matter anymore? He's dead."

She started to cry and tried to turn away, but Bolan wasn't planning on falling for any more ploys. Pretty or not, she was in this up to her eyeballs and he was going to find out what she knew.

"I know Trenton's dead," he said. "That's what happens when you get involved with the Mafia. Why don't you tell me what you know so I can put a stop to them for good?"

"I overheard a detective say that *you* killed him!" she gritted, her sorrow turning to anger in a split second.

"If I killed him, why would I show up here?" Bolan asked.

"Lacroix killed him." He let go of her arm, and she yanked it away.

As Sandra pulled a handkerchief from her purse and wiped her tear-streaked face, Bolan decided to try a different approach. "I'm sorry for your loss," he said. "Death is a hard thing."

She looked at him, then nodded and moved to a nearby chair where she sat down bonelessly. He could see the dark circles under her eyes and a faint bruise across the side of her cheek. "Talk to me, Sandra," he said. "Please."

The woman was silent for a moment longer, then took a deep, wavering breath, nodded to herself and laughed weakly. "My brother is—was—an idiot. Once Costello got to him, Trenton couldn't see that it would end badly. All he could see were Costello's big plans and how much money he would be paid to help out."

"What was Costello planning that had him so excited?"

"I'm not sure," she said, "but Trenton kept saying that we were going to be rich and that he would be able to take me away from here."

Bolan watched her carefully, then said, "I think you're lying to me. You know more than you're saying."

"Think what you want. All we talked about was getting out of New Orleans. Trenton said we could go to the Mediterranean or the Caribbean and spend the rest of our lives soaking up the sun on some beach. He said we'd be safe there, and that we'd never come back to this horrible city again." She sniffled once more. "He could only see the money Costello was paying him, but not the cost."

"You had to know he'd gotten himself into something criminal. He was in the dirt up to his armpits. Why didn't you get involved or turn him in?" he asked.

"He's my brother," she said. "You don't rat out your brother." She shrugged. "Besides, this is New Orleans, and there's no such thing as clean. Not before the hurricane and certainly not after. Haven't you figured that out yet?"

"I'm getting there," Bolan said, then stopped and looked at her. He thought about all the things he'd discovered about New Orleans and what he knew about the woman sitting in the city morgue after having seen her brother's dead body with his brains blown out. Anyone could fall prey to greed, especially secondhand. Had her involvement been indirect until the warehouse scene?

"Why did you help Costello and Salerno by leading me to the warehouse?" he asked.

"I was dating Victor off and on for the past few months," she admitted. "He's very possessive, and he told me that if I helped him, then he would make sure Trenton was taken care of." The implications of his words caught her, and she sobbed once. "I guess he kept his word. I really thought he would help us. I was a fool. Not that you believe anything that I say, and I really don't blame you."

"I don't trust you," he said. "Not yet. But tell me what you do know, and I'll do what I can to help your case."

"My case?" she asked. "What case?"

"The case that will be filed against you when all of this comes out," he said. "You'll be arrested, and at the very least charged with conspiracy. And since people like Costello aren't interested in helping out people like you, you'll either die in jail or be sent to prison for years."

Sandra stared at him for several long seconds, then barked out a laugh. "Wow," she said when she caught her breath, "you don't pull punches, do you?"

"I find it saves time," Bolan said. "So, will you tell me what you know or should I just haul you in right now?"

"I tried to get you killed. Why would you help me?"

"Because sometimes people get into situations that they

can't see a good way out of, and I believe that's what you did. So, do you know something that can help?"

She blew her nose and then nodded. "The bank," she said.

"What about the bank?"

"Trenton told me that if anything ever happened to him, I was to get the key for his safe-deposit box and take what I found there. He said it would help me. I always thought it would be money to help me get away, but maybe it's something else."

Bolan reached down and pulled her to her feet. "If you're lying to me or if this is another setup…" he growled.

"I'm not!" she said. "What do I have to gain by lying? I'm scared, Marshal Cooper. I'll help if I can. I think I'm a dead woman anyway."

Bolan watched her body language carefully, looking for signs that she was lying or hiding something, but didn't detect anything. "All right," he said. "My gut says you're telling the truth, but that doesn't mean I can't be wrong. You don't get another chance. The second you show that you're still playing both sides, I'll drop you like a rabid dog."

She nodded her head back and forth so fast it looked like she was having a seizure. "Yes, yes, I understand, I mean, I won't, it's not…" She was starting to babble.

"Let's go to the bank, Sandra," he said. "Maybe what we find will save your life."

THE BANK Trenton Smythe used was close enough that they didn't have to drive. Bolan left his SUV where he'd parked it, and they walked after Sandra admitted to having the key to the safe-deposit box in her purse.

"You were headed there next, weren't you?" Bolan asked. "Take the money and run, right?"

"What would you do in my place?" she snapped.

She had a point, Bolan thought, so he kept silent the rest of the way, watching her and keeping his eyes open for any hint of betrayal. This was a woman being pulled in multiple directions, so there was no predicting which way she'd eventually go. They reached the bank without incident. Bolan held the door open for her and they walked inside. The bank was fairly busy, with people coming and going, making it difficult to watch for traps. It was a risk he'd have to take, he knew. The Executioner was out of leads, and the safe-deposit box was the only game in town.

The lazy late-afternoon sun was slowly setting, and the humid warmth of the day made people move with a languid pace that was almost infuriating. Sandra pulled the key from her purse and walked to the desk of one of the account executives. The man recognized her immediately and pulled her into a tight hug. Sandra cried briefly in his arms but finally pushed away.

"So you've heard, Bradley," she said.

"Of course," the man named Bradley replied. "It's all over the news."

"I haven't seen it yet," she said. She held up the key. "Trenton said that I would need to get into his safe-deposit box right away if something ever happened to him and that I was authorized. I know it seems insensitive, but I have a feeling he wouldn't have told me that unless it was important."

"Perhaps he updated his will," the man guessed. "Or has some other documents that will help you in this difficult time."

"I don't know," she said. "I'm just doing what he wanted me to do."

"Of course," Bradley said. "Right this way." He paused and gave Bolan the once-over. "Does your friend want to wait in the lobby?"

Bolan glared at her.

"No, that's not necessary," she said. "I want him with me for this."

They followed Bradley into the vault after he'd retrieved the necessary master key. Then he slid his key into the lock, and Sandra followed with hers. She removed the box, and he led them to a small separate room for privacy.

"If you need anything else or if there's anything I can do, let me know," he said, and when Sandra thanked him, Bradley left them in peace.

Sandra opened the box, while Bolan looked on. Inside was a small stack of cash, maybe a total of five thousand dollars, and an envelope. He nodded and she pulled out the cash and the envelope. Before she could say or do anything else, Bolan reached forward and plucked the envelope out of her hand, opened it and a small flash drive slipped onto the table. It was marked as a two gigabyte drive, which was a lot of data.

"What do you think's on it?" she asked.

"Hopefully something that will help get you out of this mess and give me the information I need." He considered his situation for several moments, then said, "I'm going to have to go back to my hotel. I hid my computer there, and there's a good chance the cops didn't find it."

"Why not just use any computer?" she asked. "There's an internet café right down the street!"

"Because your brother wasn't dumb enough to leave this information unencrypted," Bolan said, slipping the drive into his pocket. "I'm going to need some special software to read the information that's on it."

She looked like she wanted to protest, but before she could say anything Bolan told her they were done and it was time to go moving. Looking dejected, Sandra closed the box and zipped up her purse with the cash safely tucked inside.

They walked out of the vault and saw that several police

cars had pulled up outside the bank, their lights flashing. Bradley stepped up to them and smiled.

"I think the officers outside would like to have a word with your friend, Sandra," he said. "Maybe you should wait here with me."

10

"Bradley, what have you done?" Sandra asked.

"I knew something was wrong when I saw how this man was treating you," he said defensively. "I suspected he was forcing you to open your brother's safe-deposit box."

Bolan shot a look at Sandra. "Don't blame me," she said. "I didn't do anything."

"Well, Bradley, it appears you've stuck your nose in where it doesn't belong," Bolan said. Without warning, he reached out with one long arm and grabbed Bradley by the back of his collar, turned him around and pushed him in front of them as they moved toward the bank lobby.

"Come on," he said to Sandra. "We've got to move!"

"To where?" she asked, following in his wake.

Bolan kept his own counsel until they reached the lobby, which had emptied out in a hurry. The last few customers were running for the doors, not knowing what was going on, but inspired by the sudden appearance of several police cars sprouting flashing lights, wailing sirens and armed law enforcement. Not even slowing, the soldier moved toward the exit.

"Are you crazy?" she yelled. "We can't go out there unarmed!"

"Who said I was unarmed?" he muttered, then turned

and added, "Stay behind me and keep up. If you fall behind, they'll gun you down in a second."

Shoving the terrified Bradley out the door in front of him with his left hand, Bolan pulled the Desert Eagle out of its holster rig with his right. There were enough people around to create an almost perfect phalanx of bodies in front of him, and the cops hadn't yet spotted him when he opened fire.

His first round boomed over Bradley's ear and the man screamed again, trying to fall to the ground, but Bolan held him upright. The .44-caliber round slammed into the windshield of a police cruiser, spraying safety glass. There was a moment of pure, almost clean silence, before all hell really broke loose.

The customers fleeing the bank began screaming and running in all directions, while the police tried desperately to find a target in the wave of people. Bolan was grateful they didn't fire, but it was a calculated risk at best. Maybe his luck was finally turning for the better. They reached the corner of the building and went around it, then Bolan stopped.

"Hold here one moment," he said to Sandra.

He yanked the nearly limp Bradley to his feet and spun him. "You nearly got a lot of innocent people killed," he said. The man stammered an explanation, white-faced, and Bolan shook his head in disgust.

"Get out of here," he said, shoving the man back in the direction of the bank. Bradley stumbled, nearly fell, found his feet and ran like the Devil was chasing him.

Bolan risked a quick look around the corner and saw several cops heading their way. "Time to go," he said, grabbing Sandra's hand. They'd almost made the end of the alley when the cops began firing. Bolan spun and fired several rounds of cover fire as they went around the corner, running for their lives.

With Bolan leading the way, they quickly disappeared

into the numerous alleyways in the French Quarter. He didn't think the police would chase them for an extended period of time, and he was right. He came to a stop and told Sandra to catch her breath. Somehow, she'd managed to keep up and keep her mouth shut the whole time—Bolan's assessment of her went up a notch.

Once her breathing was under control, Sandra knelt and leaned against a wall. "What do we do now?" she asked.

"We've got to find out what's on that flash drive," Bolan said. "Which means getting my computer back."

"And you're sure we can't open it on any other computer?"

"No, I'm not sure," he admitted. "But like I said, your brother wasn't an idiot. My guess is that he knew you'd want to use this as a bargaining chip with the authorities if something happened to him. He had to have known that there was no way Salerno or Costello would let you go, but he also had to protect what was on here in case one of them somehow got hold of it. I'm betting the files are heavily encrypted, which means we need my computer."

"How are you going to do that? Every cop in New Orleans is looking for you."

"I have a friend," he said.

Bolan pulled out his cell phone and dialed the number Remy had given him. After a few rings, the ex-Navy SEAL answered. Bolan quickly filled him in on the situation and the help he needed.

"The sun goes down in about a half hour or so," Remy told him. "I'll need an hour, maybe a little longer, after that to get it done."

"That works for me," Bolan said. "Call when you've got it and we'll set up a meet."

"Done," Remy said, then broke the connection.

Sandra had heard only Bolan's side of the conversation,

but seemed satisfied that he'd arranged something. "What next?" she asked.

"We eat," Bolan said. "I'm starved."

"How can you eat at a time like this?" she asked.

"Because I'm hungry," he said. "Do you know a place nearby?"

"Are you serious?" she asked. "We're *wanted*. Everyone's looking for us. Someone will see us and tell Costello, and then he will come and we will be dead." She'd started babbling again, and Bolan sighed.

"People see what they want to see," he said. "What they expect to see. You don't think they have wanted posters of us in the restaurant, do you? We'll be fine. Now, where's a decent place to eat?"

THE RESTAURANT she took him to wasn't particularly fancy, but the moment Bolan opened the door, he felt his stomach rumble. It smelled great. He picked out a booth near the back, and after brief stops in the restroom to clean up, both of them got comfortable. To any outside observer, they'd look like an ordinary couple having dinner. Bolan had learned long ago that skipping meals wasn't something a man could do consistently and still perform at a high level. He also knew that what he'd said to Sandra was true. People saw what they wanted and expected to see. Sitting in a diner, people weren't looking for fugitives from justice. Not even police officers typically did that, though they did tend to be a bit more observant than the average patron.

Both of them ordered deep-fried soft-shell crabs, with a cup of crawfish-and-sausage gumbo on the side. The server took their order, brought out water and a loaf of bread and told them their food would be ready shortly. They remained silent, each wrapped up in his or her own thoughts, until their meal arrived. Bolan ordered a cold beer to go with his, and Sandra did the same, picking out a local amber brew she'd had before.

"So tell me more about the old Mob Family that used to populate New Orleans."

"What else do you want to know?"

"I want to know why you know. Are you a history major or something?"

"No. I work in a bank downtown. I help people get mortgages. Very boring. I started researching the crime stuff when I realized that something was off. You see things on TV and they seem so glamorous. The reason I remembered the barrel murder was because it was about the most unglamorous way to die I had ever read. But the whole thing seems weird, you know?"

"What's that?"

"The Matrangas were in power for so long and had bumped their only rival. With them out of the way, you would think that the official activity would have happened sooner than Costello. I don't know. I think the timing after the storm and the whole thing is interesting. Maybe he was just looking for an opening to start the business up."

Still, Sandra remained stiff and stopped talking while they ate. He thought about what she said. The timing of the resurgence was convenient to say the least. With the federal supports coming in, one would think it would be less likely for organized crime to rear its ugly head. Bolan finished his main course, then ordered a piece of key lime pie and coffee. As he finished, he noticed she was staring at him.

"What is it?" he asked.

"You've got quite an appetite," she said. "I'm not sure I've ever seen a grown man put away that much food in one sitting."

He'd noticed that her plate was still more than half-full when the server took it away. Now she was gingerly sipping at a glass of iced tea. "It's been a long couple of days," he said quietly. "Food is the source of strength and energy, and I don't know when I'll have a chance to eat again."

She nodded, but he could tell her thoughts were elsewhere. He let her work herself up to it, and she finally said, "So tell me about yourself Marshal Cooper."

"No," he said shortly. "It doesn't work that way."

"Why not?" she asked. "You've dragged me through a shootout with the police and, however you spin it, my brother is dead because you were poking around down here. The least you could do is tell me something about the man responsible for so much misery."

Bolan sighed. "Look, Sandra. We aren't friends, and I'm keeping you with me because until this is over, I'm your best chance of staying alive long enough to get out of the mess you're in. I'm sorry about your brother, but he got himself killed by willfully getting involved with the wrong sort of people. And the only person causing real misery down here is Costello. This little organization he has going on is wrecking a lot of lives. And your brother—whether you admit it or not—was a big part of the reason that Costello has been able to terrorize as much as he has." Bolan leaned back and sipped his coffee, then added, "Another thing. People keeping secrets when it might mean life or death, they're only helping the bad guys like Costello. People like you."

"Me?" she asked. "I've told you everything."

"Not everything," he said.

"So what is it you think I know?" she asked, the bitterness obvious in her voice.

Bolan smiled grimly. "The files on that flash drive your brother left could have all kinds of protections on them—and probably do. At least one of them will be a password. I can take care of the encryption, but the password for the drive itself may be tricky. What is the password going to be?"

"How would I know?" she asked.

"Because he would make sure that you knew or could at least figure it out," he said. "Was there a nickname he called you or a place where you went to camp, maybe a name that was special to the two of you?"

Sandra blushed and took another sip of her tea.

"See," he said. "You do know something more. What is it?"

"Beau Breaker," she said, blushing furiously.

"What?" he said.

"Fine," she said. "Back when I was in high school I had a lot of boyfriends. Most of the guys I dated were athletes of one kind or another. It seemed like every time I broke up with one they would, you know, end up broken in some way. But it wasn't my fault. They'd get hurt in competition or at practice or even at home, but none of that mattered to anyone. It was just bad timing or bad luck. As I broke up with them, they'd wind up getting hurt. So I got labeled the Beau Breaker and it stuck."

"And you really think that would be it?"

"Trenton wasn't very popular, but I was," she said. "It was a stupid kid thing. The reason I thought of it was because he used it on his work computer. He showed me last week when I stopped by for lunch to tease me. He was always a good brother even when I wasn't a very good sister. I used to tease him in school, and I wouldn't let him sit next to me at lunch. I don't know, stupid thoughts on days like today."

"Let's hope you're right about the password. I don't want to lose this evidence," he said.

Bolan looked at his watch, then picked up his phone and tried to call Remy. There was no answer. He hung up the phone.

"Something's wrong," he said.

"Why do you say that?"

"Remy should have checked in already. He said an hour and a half or so, and it's been two. I'm going to go look for him. Information travels faster than the plague in this town."

"Shouldn't you give him more time?" she asked. "He's only a half-hour late."

"That's too long as it is. Guys like Remy and Rio they aren't late...ever," Bolan replied. "If he's in trouble, the longer I wait, the worse things could get." He looked at her over the rim of his coffee mug as he swallowed the last of the brew. "I'm afraid you're going to have to come with me."

"I'm not trying to get away," she protested. "I already said I'd help you however I could. Why don't you just tell me where to wait for you. That way you can focus on your friend and I don't get shot at again today."

"Because," he replied patiently, "if we're being watched and I leave you alone, you'll be dead, and I'd feel bad."

"You would not," she accused, giving up before the argument really started.

"Maybe, maybe not," he said, "but either way, you're coming along."

11

The alley behind the hotel was dirty and filled with trash. Rats skittered through the piles of refuse that contained everything from food to bottles to cast-off clothing and Mardi Gras beads. A rusted ladder ran up the side of the building to the roof.

"*This* is where you're staying?" Sandra asked. "Seriously?"

"It's cheap and anonymous," Bolan replied, looking to the ends of the alley to make sure there weren't any observers. "Not pretty, but then again, I'm not in a pretty line of work." He gestured to a stack of garbage cans and pallets. "Go hide over there," he said. "I'll be back as quick as I can."

She shook her head. "I'd rather go with you, thanks."

"Too bad," he replied. "I can't climb the ladder up to the roof, keep you from falling off when you get tired and protect us both at the same time." He gestured in the direction of the garbage cans. "Get hidden. Now."

Sandra moved toward the appointed hiding place, and Bolan gripped the rusted rungs of the ladder and hauled himself upward. After seeing several likely thugs out front, he suspected his best bet was to try to reach his room from the roof. With any luck, he'd also find Remy and be able to get them both out of the situation alive.

The building wasn't particularly tall, but eight stories was still a long climb. Halfway up, he realized that the sounds of exertion he heard weren't just coming from himself, and he stopped and looked down the ladder. Sandra was moving up behind him, a determined look on her face as she moved.

"I told you to hide," Bolan whispered.

"I'd rather die up here than be eaten by rats," she whispered back. "Get moving. If I stop, I'm screwed."

Bolan turned and kept moving—there was no time to waste arguing.

He was almost at the top when he saw a silhouette move across the rooftop. Bolan froze, pressing himself against the ladder. Sandra had to have seen it, too, as she stopped moving and kept silent. Bolan risked a glance up and saw that the person had moved to the corner of the roof. He looked down at Sandra and said, "Stay."

She nodded, and he turned and slipped onto the roof. The Executioner crept behind the person and was nearly on him when the gravel under foot slid beneath his boot and gave him away. The person spun, raising a mini-Uzi from beneath his suit coat.

Bolan didn't hesitate. He drew the Navy SEAL knife from the sheath at his back, stepped in and drove the blade between the man's ribs, angling it upward. His left hand moved up and covered the man's mouth before he could utter a sound. The sentry twitched, but the struggle was almost over before it began. Bolan lowered the corpse to the roof, then turned and went back to the ladder.

Looking down, he saw that Sandra was nowhere to be seen.

"Damn it," he muttered. "Where the hell is she?"

Sandra jumped out in front of him and he leaped backward, only recognizing her at the last second. "What the hell are you doing?" he whispered.

"Just trying to keep up—stay alive," she replied.

He looked at her worn face for a minute, then nodded sharply. "Come on."

He moved across the roof to the doorway that gave access to the building. A small pane of glass was set in the middle of the door, and Bolan risked a quick look. One short flight of steps down, two men were guarding the entrance to the floor his room was on.

"There are two men inside on the next landing," he said quietly to Sandra. "I'll go through, take care of them, and you follow me."

She nodded in agreement and said, "Be careful," as he braced his shoulder against the door.

With one swift move, Bolan pushed the door open and leaped down the stairs, slamming full force into the closer man, knocking him into the concrete wall. The second man spun to face the warrior, and Bolan snapped the knife free from his boot and drove it into the man's throat, cutting off his yell before he could voice it. The guard gurgled and clutched helplessly at his throat, dying before he hit the floor.

The first man was getting to his feet, still trying to clear his head. Desperate to keep the noise down, Bolan moved behind him and wrapped one strong arm around his neck. The man jerked in surprise as his airway was cut off, and he thrashed back and forth, trying to escape. Tightening his grip, Bolan crossed his left arm around the man's forehead and began to twist.

Panicked, the guard shoved backward off the wall, using his not inconsiderable weight as ballast. Bolan held on, even as his back smashed into the concrete steps and pain ratcheted through him. He gave one final jerk and the thug's neck snapped. The man's bowels and bladder let go as he died, and Bolan pushed him away, grimacing in distaste.

He turned and looked back up the stairs to see Sandra's pale face looking down at him.

"You…you killed both of them," she said.

"Part of the job," he said. "They would've done the same to me."

"I know that. It was just so…fast and brutal. And there were two of them!"

"We're not in the clear yet," he said, stretching and rubbing the bruises he knew would be forming on his lower back. "Let's get moving."

He waited for her to come down the steps, then opened the door into the hallway. His room was about halfway down, and the hall itself was empty. Bolan moved quickly to the door, motioning for Sandra to stay back and keep silent, then paused to listen. Inside, he could hear several voices, then the sound of a body absorbing a punch, followed by a soft groan of pain.

In spite of the fact that he didn't know Remy well, Bolan felt a wave of relief wash over him. Remy was in his current situation because he'd agreed to help him out, and dying should not have any part in that deal.

"Stay out here," he whispered to Sandra. "I mean it."

She nodded once in acceptance of the order, and Bolan had no choice but to take her at her word. Knowing a rush through the door might mean an instant death sentence for Remy, Bolan did the only thing he could think of. He knocked, rapping the heavy wood with his knuckles, then took a step back. Silence descended over the room.

A moment passed, then an accented voice called out, "Who is it?"

"Room service," Bolan said. "I've got your order."

"What order?" the man said, opening the door. "We didn't order any—"

His words were cut-off in midsentence as Bolan stepped

into the open doorway and slammed a kick into the man's knee. He began to crumple backward and Bolan followed immediately, driving an open palm into the man's nose, which had obviously been broken at least two or three times before. It cracked with an almost soft sound, but the blood poured freely anyway.

"Son of a bitch!" the man shouted, his voice muffled by the hands he was holding up to his face.

The room was too small to hide much of anything, and Remy was already on the move as soon as he saw that it was Bolan. Tied to a chair, he improvised by leaning forward, getting his feet under himself, then ramming the nearest Costello goon full speed. His head was his battering ram, and it had to have been hard because when it crashed into the man's crotch he screamed in agony.

Bolan shoved the already wounded man by the door backward, knowing that he had only one good leg. The thug stumbled on the weak knee and went for his gun. Bolan drew the Desert Eagle in a smooth motion and fired almost point-blank. The heavy round slammed the man backward into the wall, which was now spattered with blood and bits of tissue.

Bolan dismissed him and turned to see Remy's struggle with the two remaining thugs come to a sudden halt. In his experience, the Desert Eagle often had that kind of effect on a fight. Costello's men stopped and slowly raised their hands into the air.

"Cut him loose," Bolan told them. "Carefully." One of the men pulled a simple switchblade from his pocket and cut the twine binding Remy to the chair, which dropped to the ground with a thud. The ex-Navy SEAL stood to his full height.

"Thanks," he said. "They got the drop on me."

Bolan looked him over, and other than some good bruises,

he didn't appear much worse for the wear. "You look like you'll live," he said.

"They hit like girls," Remy said. "My baby sister punched harder than this one when she was six."

"Hey…" the guy closest to him started to say, and Remy moved so quickly that even Bolan had a tough time seeing the action. His hand flashed out in one nearly invisible motion, a knife-hand blow to the larynx. The man's eyes widened and he made a weak coughing sound as he went to his knees.

"See, now that's how you hit someone," Remy told him.

"Enough playtime," Bolan said. "The cops will be here any minute."

"You shouldn't have fired that rocket launcher you call a handgun," he replied.

Bolan shrugged. "I'm starting to run out of patience. Did you find it?"

He shook his head. "I never got that far."

"Sandra, you can come in here," Bolan called out, and she entered the room. "Close the door," he added.

She did and moved into the dimly lit room, stepping over the dead man on the floor, keeping her eyes averted. The thug left standing looked at her with his eyes wide.

"You're crazy, Sandra," he said. "Victor will kill you. You know that. He trusted you, and you go betraying him like this. Yeah, he'll kill you and he'll enjoy doing it."

"I'm done with Victor," she said. "I'm done with this whole city. I just want out. Victor killed my brother. I only ever wanted to make sure Trenton was safe. But you people would have never let him go. It took me a long time to realize that you were never going to let me go, either. I'm sick of all of this. No more killing and blood. I don't like any of it."

"You'll never make it out of this city alive," the thug said, his voice turning to ice. "Traitorous bitch. If I have to kill you myself, I'll make sure that you rest right next to your dear old brother."

Remy's arm flashed out again, and he thumped the man a good one on the temple. He staggered sideways and Remy caught him easily, then put the man in the chair he'd been tied up in moments before.

"Go ahead and tie him," Bolan said. "Sandra, come here." He moved over to the small closet and opened the door. Inside, he popped off the cover that gave access to the water pipes in the bathroom. Sticking his arm in the wall, he went in all the way up to his shoulder, found the laptop case and pulled it out. A quick search wouldn't have found it, even if the searcher had removed the panel.

He handed it back to Sandra. "Hold this, would you?" he said, giving it to her.

"Sure," she said, taking it, then moving away to give him room to stand up.

Bolan got to his feet and turned. In the few milliseconds it took him to realize what was about to happen, it was already too late. Remy's back was to the man on the floor, and he'd somehow made it to his knees and taken out a small 9 mm. He was pointing it straight at Sandra, who didn't even register the situation, because her eyes were on Bolan.

"Fucking traitor," the man snarled, and pulled the trigger.

"Look out," Bolan started to yell, but it was too late.

The sound of the weapon seemed puny, small in comparison to Bolan's own Desert Eagle, but it was more than enough to do the job. Sandra's expression was a study in confusion as her brain tried to catch up to what had just happened. Then she looked down.

The bullet had pierced the laptop case with ease, passed

through the computer itself and embedded itself in her chest. She took one small step forward, then collapsed to the floor in a limp heap.

12

Remy lashed out with one massive leg and kicked the gun from the man's hand, breaking bones in the process. The thug howled, but that didn't slow the ex-Navy SEAL, who spun away from the man he'd just tied to the chair, yanked the shooter up from the floor and broke his neck with an audible crack that was nearly as loud as the gunshot.

"Jesus," the other man muttered, more to himself than anyone else. "Who the hell are you people?"

Remy turned to face the last remaining thug, his face flushed with anger. "You boys are pretend bad," Remy told him in a deep voice that sounded as if it came out of the bowels of some volcano. "You play at being tough, but mostly you play dirty."

"Yeah, what of it?" he asked.

Remy jerked a thumb in Bolan's direction, then pointed at himself. "We're the real bad," he said. "And like my buddy here already said—playtime is over."

Since Remy had the thugs under control, Bolan ran to the bathroom, yanked a handful of towels off the shelf, then returned to Sandra. She'd fallen facedown on the floor, and there was no exit wound on her back.

Remy knelt next to him and together they gently rolled her over to assess the damage. Bolan pulled the remains of his laptop case away from her chest, and immediately put towels down, trying to staunch the blood.

"No exit," Remy said, "but that computer must have slowed the bullet some, reduced the impact."

Sandra's breathing was raspy, and the first towel was quickly soaking through. "She's going to need an ambulance," Bolan said.

"Every cop in town is looking for you," Remy said. "We can't just call 911."

Bolan grabbed the phone out of his pocket and punched in the number that Grady Black had given him earlier. The FBI agent answered on the second ring and Bolan quickly filled him in on what he needed, not bothering to add extra details.

"Ambulance is on the way," Bolan said, turning his attention back to Sandra. Her breathing was getting more and more shallow as her chest cavity began to fill with blood and oxygen. He tried putting on more pressure, but could feel the ribs that were broken by the bullet's passage begin to move. A strange slurping sound was coming from her wound. "Her lung has collapsed," he said. "This is going to hell in a hurry."

"Sucking chest wound," Remy said. "Hang on."

The ex-Navy SEAL got to his feet and began rummaging through the room, and when that didn't work, he tore through the door like a madman and ran down the hall. Bolan kept the pressure on as best as he could, but he knew that she was going to fade fast without help. And the Executioner realized that if he didn't get out of here soon, most likely he'd be dead or in jail.

Remy came back into the room, carrying a roll of tape and some plastic wrap. "Had to find the housekeeping closet on this floor," he said. "Hold her still."

Bolan held her firmly while Remy taped the plastic down

over three sides of the wound, leaving a tiny section uncovered. "That should help some," he said. "The air can escape, but it won't get sucked down to where it doesn't belong."

"Guard the door," Bolan said. "We don't know who will get here first, and I'm not up to being arrested." Through the windows, he could hear the pelting siren of an ambulance and several long minutes later, two paramedics came through the door, followed by Grady Black.

The paramedics moved Bolan out of the way and began treating Sandra immediately. They knew she needed a hospital and a surgeon as fast as possible, and they didn't waste valuable time asking Bolan questions. Once they inserted two large bore IVs, they were making their way out of the room.

After introducing himself to Remy, Black gave the room a quick once-over and shook his head. "You're a force of destruction, Cooper," he said. "But you'd better get a move on. It took the city cops a couple of extra minutes to decide who to send this way, but they're en route and will be here any minute."

"How do you plan to keep her safe?" Bolan asked, watching as Sandra was wheeled out of the room.

"The paramedics and the hospital are going to report that she's a nineteen-year-old kid with a gang history. It won't stay that way long, but it will give us time to take care of whatever is going on."

He nodded. "Is Lacroix still in custody?"

"Yeah, but unless we get some hard evidence against Costello I'm going to have to turn him over to the DA, and the most they'll charge him with is Smythe's murder. And with as many fingers as are in the legal pie down here, it will never stick." He looked over at the man tied to the chair. "I'm not interested in the little fish. I want the big one in this case."

"I think this may have what you want," Bolan said. He pulled out the flash drive they'd removed from the safe-deposit box. "I was coming here to get my laptop and decrypt it, but my computer got demolished in this chaos, so you're going to have to handle it from here."

"I've got a good guy on my team who can take care of any encryption and remove any booby trap that might destroy documents. Is the drive password protected?" Black asked.

"Probably," he said. "If so, try Beau Breaker for the password."

"Beau Breaker?" he asked.

"Too long a story to get into," Bolan said, hearing the police sirens closing in on the building. "We've got to go."

"Stay in touch, Cooper," Black said. "And stay alive."

"I'll do my best," he said, then turned to Remy. "Let's get going."

"I think we need to take you someplace out of the way while you work on your plan," Remy said. "We can go into the swamp. No one will find us there."

"So far, I haven't really enjoyed my swamp time," Bolan said, following the giant man into the hallway.

"It's almost alligator-free," Remy replied. "Most of the time."

NICK COSTELLO hung up the phone and lowered his aching head into his hands. One of his informants inside the local FBI office had just informed him about the flash drive that Smythe had left for his sister to find, and then she'd immediately given it to this Cooper character, who'd then given it to FBI Special Agent Grady Black. He was one of the agents he didn't have in his pocket yet.

"Victor," he said, "I told you that woman was trouble, didn't I?"

"Yeah, boss, you did," Victor Salerno replied. "Everything's just happened so damn fast. I haven't had time to deal with her yet."

"Forget her for now," he said. "We've got other problems."

Nick didn't see himself as the kind of man to give in to panic, but at the rate things were collapsing, no one could blame him if he had some kind of a nervous breakdown. The evidence that would sink him was mounting rapidly, he was losing men left and right, and every time he thought he had the noose around Cooper's neck, the man slipped through it like a greased pig.

"This guy Cooper has gone past being an irritation," Nick said. "We're going to go after him with everything we've got. I want him dead."

"Okay," Salerno said, "I agree with you. But we still have a shipment to see to."

"The shipment can wait!" Nick yelled, standing up so fast his chair fell over behind him. "If we don't get rid of this guy and whatever evidence Smythe left on that drive, the shipment won't matter. We'll both be in jail or dead!"

Salerno held up his one good arm. "All right, Nick," he said. "All right. Marshal Cooper first, then."

"Get it handled," Nick shouted. "I'm done with the games, you get me? I want him dead and out of the way. Tonight."

Clearly Salerno knew when to stop talking and start walking because he just nodded, turned and left the room quickly. Nick picked up his chair and sat down. Nothing was going right—the marshal downstairs still hadn't given him what he wanted, and his whole empire seemed to be crumbling before his eyes. He'd waited too long for all of this to come together. This game was supposed to help him get clear of everything, and if it didn't change directions fast it was just going to put more names on the list of people who wanted him dead.

All because of one guy named Cooper. Who the hell was this guy?

REMY AND BOLAN pulled up to the hidden island that enclosed the secluded shack. Running an airboat in the dark of night took a lot of skill, but the ex-SEAL handled it with aplomb, guiding them without hesitation. Once Remy had tied off the airboat, both men made their way back into the interior, pushing the vines and moss out of their way as they went. It was a good spot to lie low, but it lacked a lot of amenities. Still, Bolan had everything he needed for the moment, and the most important thing was to put together a plan for dealing with Costello.

Once they were inside, Remy offered chicory coffee and brewed up a pot, then poured each of them a cup. Neither man wanted cream or sweetener, and despite the humid night heat, Bolan thought that the coffee felt good going down. They sat at the small kitchen table for a little bit, just resting and getting their bearings. Finally, the soldier cleared his throat. "Okay, my friend, we're deep in it, and I've got a question for you."

"Go ahead," Remy answered.

"What's your story?"

"What do you mean?" Remy asked.

"All this," Bolan said. He pointed around the room and then looked back at Remy. "This is not a hideout. This is where you're living. Why?"

"I suppose you'll just have your friends look it up anyway," he said. "If you haven't already."

Bolan shook his head. "No, I haven't. And if you tell me to stay the hell out of your business, I will. It's your life. But since you saved my ass from the gators, and you've kept on helping even when it got more than a little dangerous for you, I figure I can at least ask. I like to know who I'm working with." He finished off his coffee. "Besides, I saw how you handled yourself back at the hotel. Why are you hiding—a man with your skills?"

Remy put his mug on the table and sighed. "I loved being a SEAL, man. There was something about it, you know? That ability to do things that others never had the skills or the balls to get done. I was good at it, too."

"I bet," Bolan said.

"Anyway," he continued as though he hadn't heard a word, "my last operation was over in Iraq. A shadow op that was FUBAR from start to finish. We had some intel that one of the private military companies doing security over there was torturing prisoners. Not really that big of surprise. It's war and it happens. But the bigger problem was that the guy running the show was selling information to other terrorist groups, and feeding out false information to our guys. People were getting killed. Our people."

Bolan kept his mouth shut, and just listened.

"Long story short, I got sent into their little prison camp on a solo recon. That's all it was supposed to be. If we confirmed, we'd do a full team strike that night." He shook his head. "I've seen things that shoulda turned my hair white and done things that I'm not proud of, but the way this guy was running his camp… It made the Vietcong look like angels of mercy."

Bolan pitched his voice low. "Lost it?"

"Totally," Remy said. "My own crew had to come in unprepped, but we fragged that whole place, got the prisoners out. I killed the main guy myself. CNN reported that the prison camp was attacked by suicide bombers."

"You did your job," Bolan said, "and got rid of a scumbag."

"Yeah, but I didn't join the Navy or the SEALs so I could kill Americans. The whole thing got covered up and those bastards were lauded as heroes for their service." He shrugged. "I knew I needed to get away."

"And you couldn't have chosen a nice sandy beach somewhere? Why an alligator infested swamp?"

"I wanted to get away from people. No one wants to come out here. At least the gators are honest. They want their next meal, but beyond that they haven't a care in the world. I can deal with an honest killer. It's the deceit and the lies that get to me more than anything. You start wondering about the guy cutting the orders, and as a soldier you can't do that. You have to believe that orders are from a good place that understands what they are asking of their men in the field. As a soldier, you can't decide which order you're going to follow."

"I suppose you want my story," Bolan said.

"I was a SEAL, remember? I understand that you'll tell me what I need to know. We all have a story."

"Well, Remy," Bolan said, "I can't speak for anyone else, but I appreciate your service with or without the uniform. If we make it out of this particular mess alive, if you want to go back into a life of this kind of service I can help make arrangements for you. I know it may not be what you wanted there for a while, but you're good and you know the stakes. Either way, for my book, you've made an ally. I'll never forget what I owe you."

"You don't owe me, Cooper. I may have saved your life, but you gave me mine back. You helped me remember that there are things that are worth fighting for."

13

Grady Black had spent long enough in New Orleans to know that the few times hope floated, it was usually eaten by an unseen gator rising out of the muck. His computer sciences tech had decrypted the flash drive fairly easily, especially with the odd "Beau Breaker" password that let him gain access. He'd handed it off to Black a couple of minutes ago, with a quiet, "Easy as pie," and returned to his station to shut down for the night. He'd been nice enough to stay late at Black's request.

He slipped the drive into an open USB port and waited for his system to access it, and create a file folder on his desktop. Before Black even opened the contents, he made a copy and shipped it to an off-site server storage that he paid for out of his own pocket. He suspected that Costello had people on his payroll in the FBI office, and he didn't want to risk whatever the contents were on a single system. Once he'd confirmed the transfer, he took a deep breath and opened the folder. There were about a dozen individual files, most of them spreadsheets. He clicked on the one labeled FINANCIALS and began to read.

After several minutes, Black selected the most recent one, which was labeled SHIPPING. Once he'd scanned the contents of that one, he shook his head in disbelief. There was enough in the financials file alone to put Costello and La-croix and almost everyone else connected to them away for a long, long time. Bribes, payoffs, account numbers, holding company names. It was all there in black and white, and the FBI agent wondered if Smythe was braver than anyone had given him credit for. If Costello had known how much Smythe knew… Black shook his head once more.

The shipping file was the most worrisome. It was clear that Costello was not only stealing FEMA supplies and then charging the government for its own materials, but he was also doing a booming business in illegal weapons. There was a key on the bottom of the page indicating what each crate was labeled and what it actually contained. Almost all of the weapons were either Israeli or Russian, which seemed very odd, considering Costello's Italian connections.

Still, Black had more than enough to start making arrests. Lots of arrests. He closed the file windows and sat back in his chair. With a little luck, busting this case would be enough to get him a transfer to a better office—maybe someplace less humid. None of it would matter, he reminded himself, if he couldn't actually make the arrests and get the bad guys and the evidence into court. The connections to Israel and Russia gave the whole thing international implications, too, and if he ever wanted a promotion out of here, he was going to have to get started. The real work was only beginning.

He picked up the black phone on his desk and punched the button for his boss's office. When he answered, Black said, "Glad you're still in, sir. I have something very interesting."

"I was just about to go home, Agent Black," Len Perotti said. "What is it?"

"I just received enough evidence to put Costello, La-croix and everyone connected to them away for the rest of their lives. This is the break we've been looking for in these cases."

"Are you certain?" he snapped. "I don't want us going off on some kind of wild-goose chase. We've got enough real cases, you know."

"Sir, I know you're mad as hell about my bringing Lacroix in, but I heard him confess to murder. And we've been looking for something solid on Costello for a long time. Trust me. There's more than enough here to put them all away for good. I have financial information and details on their weapons smuggling. This is the real deal, sir."

"All right," Perotti said. "Send it to my screen and let me have a look at it."

"Right away," he said.

"Oh, and Agent Black?"

"Sir?"

"Until I've had a chance to look at what you've got, you keep quiet and stay in the office. Until you hear back from me, I don't want you doing a thing. If what you've got is as big as you think, we want to plan our next steps very carefully."

"I understand, sir," Black said, then hung up the phone. He set up the file transfer on his computer and sent the decrypted files directly to his boss's screen. Black took off his jacket and rolled up the sleeves of his pinstriped dress shirt. He started pulling out maps and the other things he would need for the briefing. Hopefully, they'd be able to find a judge willing to issue warrants this night.

REMY PULLED OUT a map of the New Orleans area and spread it on the table. Bolan propped a foot on the chair, sipping his coffee as he leaned in while Remy pointed out the two most likely locations where Costello could be holding Rio.

"The main compound is here. It's a large place, used to be an old plantation or something. He tore down the original house and built this one, with a fenced perimeter and plenty of guards all of the time. It runs right along the swamp, and then there is the main road coming in and out that can split off pretty fast," he said, indicating an area several miles from Remy's shack. "That's the most likely place."

"What's the other one?" Bolan asked.

Remy pointed to another spot on the map. "There's been a lot of traffic in this part of the swamp," he said. "I think it's just a shipping point for him, but it's possible Costello's got a building of some kind there. I've never checked it out close enough to be certain, but if I had to put money on it I would say your friend is at the compound. They say he likes to make people talk, and he wouldn't want to make the effort of traveling out into the swamp every day."

Bolan considered it and nodded. "I've known a lot of mafiosi. They like their comforts, and appearance is everything. If Rio's still alive, he'll be somewhere in the main compound. My guess would be that Costello's never even been to the other place where you've seen his men moving about. That would actually mean getting out in the muck, and he really doesn't sound like the type."

"That makes sense," Remy said. "He's got a real advantage in this part of the world. There are a lot of places to hide. Of course, that's a disadvantage, too. It makes sneaking up on him that much easier."

Bolan smiled grimly. "Then we'll play to that," he said. "With any luck, we can be on top of him before he knows we're even there."

"You said that the weapons were in large crates."

"Yeah, why?"

Remy looked down at the map again and traced out two routes.

"Because those would need a pretty good-size boat, and most boats with any kind of draft don't make it through the swamp, they get hung up. Even small skiffs get abandoned regularly because they get snagged. And there aren't a lot of people who are willing to swim under their boats here to get them loose."

Outside there was a quiet thud and a splash from the water.

Remy saw his reaction. "Probably just ol' Gramps," he said. "Big gator that I've seen around here, about sixteen feet long or so. He comes by for a visit every now and again."

"You visit with the alligators," he said.

"Mostly I just try to stay out of their way," he said. "But it never hurts to be neighborly. Besides when he's sitting on your front steps not a whole lot of folks are going to come knocking. He's the best kind of guard dog—I don't feed him, never had to train him and he'll eat most intruders."

Another bump was followed by a splashing sound. "*That* wasn't an alligator," Bolan whispered.

Both men moved toward the front of the cabin, and Remy peered through the small window. Through the heavy veil of moss and hanging trees, he could see three bright floodlights attached to the front end of airboats. They were pointed down, but it still allowed him to see that they had trouble. Several dogs started howling, and he ducked back down.

"How the hell did they find us?" Remy asked. "Not that it matters. There's at least three airboats that just made landfall. Men and dogs." He shrugged. "I can't tell if they're law enforcement or Costello's men."

"We can discuss it later," Bolan said. "Right now we need to get the hell out. Is there any other way out of here?"

"Yeah," the big man said. "Get your stuff and let's go."

They quickly grabbed what they needed, then moved into the small kitchen area. Remy slid the table aside, and kicked the area rug beneath it out of the way. Bolan saw that he'd revealed yet another trapdoor, not unlike the one where he kept his extra weapons. But this one was a tunnel.

"Perfect," Bolan started to say, then looked closer. It was filled with water. "Okay, less than perfect."

Bolan pulled open the door and leaned back when the water splashed.

"It's a water tunnel," Remy rumbled. "Hope you're a good swimmer."

"Do I have a choice?" Bolan asked.

"Not really," he replied.

Remy moved away from the trapdoor and lifted a floor panel in the kitchen. Inside were two car batteries, a timer and a set of wires. Remy connected the wires and the timer to the batteries, then said, "I'm ready."

Bolan raised an eyebrow with the unspoken question and he added, "Just a couple of surprises for our friends."

THE HAZE THAT HAD finally and blessedly taken Rio into painless oblivion began to dissipate. His eyes flickered open and while a part of him desperately wanted to fade back into that place, he forced himself to open them all the way and wake up. He peered around the room and saw that it was empty, and he didn't hear anyone on the steps or walking the floor above his head. Part of him was blissfully aware that the torture was not about to begin again, but the tired part of his soul wished that they would just kill him if that was what they were planning to do. Rio shook his head trying to physically remove the depressing thoughts. He was never one to sit and feel sorry for himself, and he wasn't about to start now.

The marshal tried moving his wrists, but found they were still tied. He twisted his left wrist, trying to adjust his position, and realized that hand was nearly loose. The sweat and blood and his thrashing had loosened and stretched the heavy binding. He moved the hand again to test the mobility, and with each movement the restraint seemed to loosen a little more. Finally fully conscious, he looked at the rope and began to maneuver his wrist back and forth, looking for the one motion that would free his hand. Finally the rope gave enough to slide his fist through. That gave him enough freedom to roll onto his side and reach his right hand, which he quickly freed.

Suddenly desperate for speed, Rio sat up and untied his feet, then swung his legs off the table and tried to stand. He almost immediately crumpled to the ground. His head spun, and his devastated knee wouldn't support his weight. He had to shake off the darkness that tried to ensnare him again. Over the past few days the blackouts had been a mercy, but this was not the time to succumb to oblivion. His clothing was in a heap on the floor, and he dragged himself over to the small pile and got dressed. He started feeling more human the minute the cotton touched his skin.

Using the stainless-steel table he'd been tortured on, he pulled himself up, but couldn't bear weight on his injured leg. Rio looked around the room for something to support himself with, but found nothing. Knowing he had no choice and that time was crucial, he eased himself back to the floor and began to crawl, dragging his leg behind him, each movement a special agony. When he reached the stairs, he was covered in sweat, but he forced himself to keep going. Using the handrail to support himself, he got to his feet once more and propelled his battered body up the stairs. At the top he paused, listening for any sound from his captors, but the house remained silent and still.

Rio opened the door and entered a kitchen area, strangely pleased to find that there was a chair close enough to use as a pseudo-walker. He grabbed hold of it and made his way to the refrigerator. Inside, there was bottled water. He took one and drank it almost without stopping. His body was crying out for more, but he resisted, knowing that he'd already consumed too much, too fast. He dug through the refrigerator and found some sliced roast beef and cheese, both of which he took, along with another bottle of water. He ate quickly, gobbling down the food and more water as fast as he could. He knew he shouldn't delay making his escape, but his body needed sustenance. Costello hadn't been a very generous host and had little interest in feeding or giving a beverage to his game room guest.

As soon as he finished, Rio used the chair to get to the back door, which led out of the kitchen and into a small patio area. There was a short spade shovel leaning against the house, and Rio grabbed it and used it as a makeshift cane. Keeping as much of his weight as possible off his injured knee, he moved away from the house and into the trees surrounding the property. Most of them were some kind of willow or Spanish moss and as soon as he reached cover, he stopped again to rest. Several times, his overburdened stomach threatened to rebel, but Rio forced himself to breath and keep everything down. He was going to need all his strength. The area looked remote and the trees quickly turned into swamp.

Sudden shouts made him flinch. His absence had been discovered! His heart raced as he saw men running into the compound. There was no way for him to use the small, single lane road that led away from the property.

His only choice was to go into the swamp and pray he could make it out alive.

14

"How long before they get here?" Bolan asked, just on the verge of going through the trapdoor.

Remy walked back over to the window and took another quick look. "They're moving pretty slow, being cautious. Five minutes, maybe a little longer. Why?"

"We need time to get through the tunnel," Bolan said. "And it wouldn't hurt to thin their ranks a little either."

Remy grinned. "What'd you have in mind?" he asked. Bolan quickly sketched his idea and they agreed. Remy disconnected the timer from his "surprise," and then they slipped out of the shack and into the darkness, with each of them taking a slightly different angle toward the men starting to spread out on the thin strip of land to begin their search.

Bolan's idea was simple. If he and Remy came at them from each side, taking out those on the edge of the search party, it would quickly cause chaos and confusion. They'd have to reel everyone in closer, which in turn would cause them to be more bunched up when they reached the shack. With any luck at all, there wouldn't be anyone left to pursue them.

Bolan crept through the trees, letting the hanging branches and moss do most of the work of keeping him concealed. He could hear the quiet whispers of the men as they tried to get organized to sweep the island. He moved in closer and paused, letting his eyes adjust and pick out the forms. They had three or four dogs, which could be a problem, but the air was humid and the swamp filled with swirling scents.

He looked at his watch and checked the time. Bolan figured that Remy should be in position on the far right end of their line, so he moved silently down to the far left. As he moved in, Bolan realized that the men were a mix of off-duty law enforcement and typical Mafia enforcers, most of whom looked really out of their element in the swamp. A voice called from the center of the line for everyone to get ready.

Bolan stopped. The voice was familiar, and it took him a moment to place it—Victor Salerno. He silently cursed that the man was in the middle of the line. Getting to him might still be possible, but more than likely, it would ruin the plan he and Remy had already agreed on.

The man closest to Bolan was staring back toward the center of the line, waiting for the go order. The next closest was a good ten, maybe twelve feet away. Bolan moved down to the edge of the water. He heard a hiss and another splash, and turned to see ol' Gramps slink into the water. Bolan then moved up and crept behind the man. In a flash, he yanked him backward, plunging the SEAL Combat Knife up and between his ribs. The man let out a soft, surprised grunt, but no more as the air leaked out of his lungs and the blade pierced his heart.

With a final, savage twist of the blade, Bolan turned his nameless foe loose, dropping him into the water. Ol' Gramps moved in and found his dinner, his large jaws wrapping around the man's limp leg and pulling him underwater. Using the darkness as cover, Bolan moved away.

The next man in line turned to the sound. "Tommy, you all right?" he whispered, taking several steps in that direction. His stylish clothes were out of place, and ruined by the swamp. With each step he looked back down at his feet mumbling about the injustice of his shoes getting ruined.

When there wasn't an answer, he moved closer to the water again. "Tommy?"

Bolan moved once more, this time coming in from the side. The blade flashed once, opening up a long gash in the man's throat and severing his windpipe. He tried to scream for help, holding his hands up to his throat, his eyes wide with shock. Dispassionately, Bolan stepped away as his second victim fell dead into the water. Ol' Gramps was going to have more than one course for dinner.

That was two, he thought, and if Remy was making similar progress, they'd already cut the group down by four and possibly more. Bolan estimated that there were less than twenty total men in the search party, so the odds were evening up slightly. He moved in to the next closest man, but this one was more aware, and was already peering into the darkness, wondering what the splashing sounds had been and where his two missing allies had gone.

The guy was backlit from the floodlights pointing at the ground. Bolan saw him open his mouth to shout a warning and decided that they'd run out of time. He drew the Desert Eagle, took aim and fired. The weapon roared his presence, the shot echoing over the water and into the swamp. The nameless thug made a brief squawking sound, his hands fluttering at the hole in his chest, then he fell dead.

"What the…" someone nearby shouted.

Salerno yelled out, "It's them! Open fire!"

Of course, there was nothing to see to open fire on, but those with Salerno gamely tried, shooting randomly and at shadows among the trees. Bolan thought he heard the sound of Remy's MK23 mixed in, and wouldn't have been the least bit surprised. He moved away quickly, making his way back to the shack. At the landing, he could still hear Salerno yelling and cursing, calling for the men to come in closer so they could do a head count.

Bolan waited for Remy at the door and a minute later he arrived. The giant black man materialized out of the swamp shadows, a grin on his face. "How'd you do?" Bolan asked.

"Three," he answered. "Maybe a fourth, but it was hard to tell for sure. You?"

"About the same," Bolan answered. They listened to the yelling on the beach subside.

"Time to go," the soldier said.

They went back inside, and Remy reset the wires and the timer, then he handed Bolan a waterproof bag. "Put your gear in that," he said. "At least we won't have to worry about mud and muck getting into our weapons that way. Water wipes off."

"True enough," Bolan said, putting his hardware into the bag, then slipping on a pair of swim goggles that Remy gave him.

"Deep breath," he said. "It's a two-minute swim."

With three big fast breaths to build up the oxygen, Remy dived headfirst into the trapdoor opening. The Executioner mimicked Remy and went in after him.

The water was so murky Bolan could barely see his own hands. The tunnel was just wide enough for one person. The soldier used the roots that encroached into the tunnel as handholds to maneuver through the narrow space. The tunnel angled slightly down, then turned to the left, and he dragged himself around the corner.

He felt a sharp tug on his shoulder, and realized that the bag carrying his weapons was hung up on a protruding root. Bolan reached back and began to yank on it, fearing he'd have to cut it loose just as help came from an unexpected source.

The shack exploded with a deep, muffled thump, and both the water and the sides of the tunnel shuddered. The shock wave dislodged his bag, and with his lungs burning, the soldier continued on, pushing harder against the walls. The explosion ruined the last of any visibility he had—he moved completely on feel.

The tunnel began to widen and slope back upward, and Bolan hoped the surface was near. He kicked hard with his legs, reaching out with his hands, and his grasping fingers slid through the mud and found the lip of the tunnel. As he tried to pull himself out, his legs became tangled in the roots along the tunnel wall. He kicked at them, but it felt like they were tightening their hold.

Bolan pulled the knife from his boot and reached back to cut through the tentacles that were trapping him. His chest was on fire, and every millisecond more made it feel like his lungs were going to explode. Spots started to fill his vision, and he could feel tingling in his limbs from the oxygen deprivation. One more cut and he was finally free.

He broke the surface, gasping for air, and saw Remy holding a finger to his lips, indicating the need for quiet. Once he caught his breath, Bolan pulled himself the rest of the way out of the tunnel. It appeared they were on another spit of land almost due south of where Remy's shack had been. From here, he could see the fire burning where the little building had been, and the smoke wafting through the moss and the trees.

"Sorry about your place," he whispered softly.

Remy shrugged, but Bolan could see that the loss weighed on his new friend. "Maybe it was time to move on anyway," the big man said. "Someplace quieter."

Bolan couldn't help but chuckle, and Remy did the same, then they moved quickly away, leaving land and wading through a short stretch of water to a stand of trees. Remy pulled the branches away to reveal a small metal boat laden with supplies. They pulled themselves up and into the little boat. The sound of angry voices carried across the dark swamp, and Bolan felt a small wave of disappointment. One of them was Salerno's.

Remy pointed through the trees, then handed Bolan an oar. Together they began to silently paddle through the trees and away from the smoke-filled air. After they were a good half mile or more away, Remy put his oar away and started the small outboard motor. They continued their escape, moving rapidly away from the little island the ex-SEAL had called home.

Bolan set down his oar and looked at his hand. A small leech had attached itself for the ride. He dislodged the unwanted passenger, then examined his arms and found two more with a similar intent. He looked over at Remy, who was also removing several leeches with one hand, while he guided the boat with the other.

Flicking the black creatures away, Bolan muttered to himself, "And he likes this place?"

IT TOOK THE BETTER part of two hours for Bolan and Remy to get out to the edge of the swamp where the Executioner had left the SUV hidden. He opened the back and changed into dry, clean clothing. The black BDU pants and gray T-shirt felt comfortable after peeling off the swamp-soaked clothes. Bolan offered an extra set to Remy, who shook his head with a smile.

"No way those'll fit me," he said.

"True, but I wanted to make the offer," Bolan said. "I'm going to get in touch with Agent Black and see where we stand." The disposable cell he'd been using was waterlogged and ruined, so he removed a new one from the compartment in the back and dialed the FBI agent's number.

It only rang twice on Bolan's end before he got an answer. "Grady Black," the voice on the other end said.

"Agent Black, it's Cooper," he said. "We're on the run again. They found Remy's shack and attacked in force. It seems like Costello has an endless army."

"How the hell did they find you out there? I looked on a map at your location in case you needed help. If Remy hadn't given me the coordinates, there would have never been a reason to be looking in that part of the swamp."

"I have no idea," he said. "Maybe Costello has people scouting the area more regularly than we guessed. Either way, tell me you got into the drive and have good news."

"I have great news," Black said. "That thing was a gold mine. We've got enough evidence to make the arrests and when it's over, they'll all be going away for a long time. The best part is it's not just one piece of evidence, it has account numbers, timelines—Smythe was very thorough."

"Excellent," Bolan said. "What's your next move?"

"I've run everything up the chain of command, and just got the green light to start putting a field team together."

Bolan considered the situation. "Are you sure that was the right move?" he asked. "Getting that many people involved?"

"No," Black admitted, "but that's the way it works, and I've got to follow protocol or the arrests won't stick. I think if something was amiss I wouldn't have been given the go-ahead. My supervisor is handpicking the team, and they should be here within the hour for the first briefing."

"All right," he said. "Just be careful and keep your eyes and ears open. We don't know how long of an arm Costello really has, and I have a strong suspicion that they have some-one on the inside there. Too many things have been kept quiet over the time period that we are looking at for it to have gone on under the FBI's radar. So let me reiterate, watch your back."

"I will," he said, then added, "I'd like to have you on the team when we go in, Cooper. If we get lucky, maybe your friend is still alive and we'll find him. None of this would have been possible without you or Remy, and you really deserve the credit."

"I wouldn't miss it," he said. "Where are you staging your men at?"

"About a half mile or so from Costello's compound. There's an old church. That's our main rendezvous point. I can send map coordinates to your GPS unit. We're scheduled to go in about ninety minutes."

"That should be fine. We'll meet you there," he said, then hung up.

Bolan quickly filled Remy in on Black's plan. "You don't have to get any more involved with this, Remy," he said. "I respect that you wanted out of this kind of business, and you've already done far more than you had to. You're not a soldier anymore, you have a choice."

The ex-SEAL was quiet for a minute, then replied, "Sometimes you can't fight who you are, and you can't ever hide from it, not really. I think you had the right of it when you told me that it sounded like I did my job and got rid of a scumbag. It shouldn't matter to me what country they come from, whether they're Americans or Russians or Italians. If I can help put an end to them hurting people, then I'll help."

Bolan nodded, pleased to see this change in the man's thinking. "All right, then," he said. "Let's go get these bastards."

15

During the night, a heavy bank of clouds had rolled in. The sky slowly lightened as the sun came up, but the early part of the day promised serious rain, and the distant rumble of thunder threatened worse than that. Bolan and Remy arrived at the church well ahead of Agent Grady Black's men. They parked the SUV in the back, where it would be out of the way of law-enforcement vehicles.

Remy glanced at the sky when they got out. "It's going to pour buckets," he said, as another roll of thunder crossed the sky.

"Agreed," Bolan side. "Let's get inside."

The church itself was an old, clapboard building, with a steeple that had long since fallen in on itself. Even in the dim light, Bolan could make out the moss-coated top of the bell that had once called people to worship. The back door was still locked, but the wood was rotted and weak. Remy shoved one broad shoulder into the door and it splintered around the lock, creaked alarmingly, then gave way completely. A loud peal of thunder shook the sky, and they stepped inside as the rain slashed down in heavy sheets.

The door led into a small room that had likely once served as a small kitchen, but was now nothing more than empty cupboards and green sinks. Another door led into the main part of the church, and they stepped through quietly. There was something about a place of worship that could make even the most hardened fighting man a little quieter. Perhaps that was why terrorist attacks on churches and mosques seemed so heinous; they were an attack on the idea of faith itself, an assault on the healing power of belief. Bolan wasn't one hundred percent certain what he believed, but whenever he stepped into a building like this one, his thoughts at least briefly turned to the idea of a world without war. He didn't think it would ever happen, the nature of humankind was far too conflict-oriented.

He and Remy saw that the pews hadn't been disturbed, so they took a seat in the last row to wait for Black and his men.

"Are you a religious man, Cooper?" Remy asked.

The soldier thought about the question for a moment, then shook his head. "Not in any traditional sense, no," he said.

"I think it's what we do," Remy said. "No matter how much it's needed or necessary, no matter how bad the bad guys are, we kill people and that takes something away from the universe. Makes it damn hard to be at peace with the world."

Bolan considered his next words carefully, then said, "What we do gives the people in the world a chance at peace, so maybe whatever the answer is, we get a pass on the formalities."

"You think?" Remy asked.

"I sure hope so," he said.

At that moment, the front doors of the church burst open with a loud bang and smoke rolled into the sanctuary. The noise of the storm had covered the approach of whoever was outside, and both men dived behind the pew and pulled their pistols.

A loud whine of feedback echoed through the building,

then a voice said, "Marshal Cooper! Remy Fountainou! The building is surrounded! Come out with your hands up and leave your weapons inside!"

"Is everyone in this entire city corrupt?" Bolan said, more to himself than to get a reply from Remy, who had crawled to the next pew over and taken a position that would cover their retreat. He held up two fingers and pointed behind Bolan.

Looking carefully through the drifting smoke, the soldier held up four fingers in reply and pointed behind the ex-Navy SEAL. He popped a smoke grenade and rolled it, banging and clanging into the center of the church. He counted a silent eight, and then the grenade popped and smoke began to billow, adding to the haze from the door explosion. Again Bolan held up four fingers and pointed behind Remy.

Staying low, knowing they only had seconds, they made eye contact. Bolan showed a count with his left hand. One. Two. Three. Both of them came up firing.

Bolan aimed his Desert Eagle over Remy's shoulder and fired three times, then dived forward, heading for the doorway into the desolate kitchen area. Remy's gun barked as well, and as the Executioner hit the ground, rolling, he turned to make sure that he could cover the big man's exit.

The officers who'd snuck into the church as part of the ambush had mostly hit the deck when they opened fire, and Bolan knew he'd accounted for at least one of them. With all the smoke it was difficult to tell, but as Remy moved forward, Bolan saw that two of them were right on their partner's heels.

"Down, Remy!" he shouted, and the big man dived forward. Bolan fired at the closer of the two men, the .44-caliber round punching into his left leg and knocking the man off his feet. The second gunner showed more sense and dived over a pew, rather than risk getting shot with a such a powerful weapon. Bolan fired two more rounds into the wooden back of the pew, showering the cowering man with sharp shards of wood and forcing him to keep his head down.

"Clear," Remy said behind him, and Bolan turned to follow. They ran out the back door of the church, already moving in a zigzag pattern as gunshots echoed behind them.

"Make for the swamp!" Remy said.

Bolan followed the big man, knowing that the hanging moss, the low branches and the pouring rain would make excellent cover. As soon as they got clear, Remy turned and checked for pursuit. "Stay out of the water here if you can," he said over his shoulder. "The gators are thicker in this part of the swamp."

Several gunners ran out of the back of the church, firing in their direction, and Bolan pushed Remy to the ground as a hail of gunfire cut through the trees. "They're firing blind, but you're big enough to make me question luck."

More gunfire erupted from the other side of the church, and a small group of men dressed in civilian clothes appeared, running around the corner and almost taking out the cops before they knew what was going on.

"Where the hell did they come from?" Remy asked.

"Must be from the compound," Bolan said. "The gang's all here."

"That's a hell of a setup for them."

"Let's keep moving," Bolan said, "and find a place to lay low. I'd rather avoid a prolonged firefight. At this point, we don't have any allies, and we're going to need some help."

They headed across a shallow patch of water, moving on a diagonal away from the church and the compound, until they came across a solid strand of trees and stopped once more. They could hear confused shouts still in the distance, but getting closer.

"Over there!" a voice called. "I think I see him."

Remy and Bolan peered through the trees, trying to figure out what was going on. Finally, Bolan spotted the small cadre of men that had been coming around the corner of the church. These definitely weren't police officers, which made them Costello's men, but whomever they were looking for wasn't the two of them. One of the men was pointing and waving his arm in the opposite direction. Bolan's gaze tracked the commotion and he saw another man in the distance, struggling through the swamp.

The falling rain and mist that rose from the swamp water obscured the form almost completely, but Bolan could tell that the person was leaning on something to support his weight. The figure stumbled, fell into the water with a splash, but levered himself back up again almost immediately.

"One of theirs, you think?" Remy asked.

Bolan shook his head, watching carefully. The rain slackened for a moment and the man turned in his direction. It was Rio. Bolan began to bolt from his hiding place, but Remy's large hand fell on his shoulder and pulled him back.

"Look," he said, pointing toward another copse of trees where several police officers were emerging.

"Damn it," he said, turning his gaze back to where Rio was struggling with several of Costello's men. At least Bolan knew the U.S. marshal was still alive, still fighting, but for the moment, the best they could do was stay put and not get captured.

It took over an hour for the police and Costello's men to leave the area. Bolan and Remy quickly made their way back to the church and got into the SUV. They drove off, winding away from the church, until the Executioner found a spot where they could pull over and talk about their next move.

Bolan had been thinking about the current situation as

he drove and had decided that he had been running around without a real plan. Or even any good intelligence on the area.

"Okay," he said. "I've been going at this all wrong. I came down here to find Rio, and somehow got caught up in who all is involved and where all the players are at instead of plowing through the problem to get to the end."

"Agreed," Remy said.

"So, I don't care about that anymore," he finished. "Our only local source of help was Grady Black, and with this ambush, he's either being held or he's dead. I don't think he was playing me false."

"Neither do I," Remy replied. "Otherwise, he wouldn't have taken Lacroix in or helped Sandra. No, I think he's probably dead. They had been able to keep him in the dark in the past, but with the new evidence he was able to move forward and that put him in the 'need to get rid of category.' He found the evidence that he's needed for a long time, and it probably cost him his life."

"So, someone in the local FBI office is dirty, too," Bolan said. "Which means even more people are hunting us and will probably try to blame us when it's discovered that Grady is missing."

"I'm with you," he said. "I don't enjoy being hunted, and maybe it's time we went to the top of the food chain, rather than the middle. I've never been much of a bottom feeder. Makes me wonder though."

"About what?"

"If Rio and Black were taken out of play, I wonder how many others sniffing around have suffered the same fate."

"I don't know, but when this is all done I'll have someone look into it."

Bolan climbed out of the seat and went to the back of the SUV and opened the hidden compartment inside.

"I'm surprised they didn't take all of your gear."

"That's why they were going to impound it," he said. "Black got it for me, so it's an FBI rig, but the security locks can withstand quite a beating. It would have been easier to open back in their own garage."

Knowing that the cell phone waves were probably being scanned by the Feds, Bolan pulled out the secure satellite phone and called Stony Man Farm.

When Brognola picked up the line, he said, "It's me."

"You're creating one hell of a stir down there, Striker. What's going on?"

Bolan sketched in the events up to that point, and finished up with the ambush at the church. "You gave me the green light on Grady Black, so I don't think he's dirty, but I do think he's probably dead," he said. "We had evidence that I gave to him to decrypt when my computer got destroyed, which he took back to the office. It looks as if the local FBI is involved. The whole thing is a mess. We had two different teams of people trying to hunt us down in the swamp. These guys are all over the place. It's like Costello has his own private army. There's no way that they were doing all of this without the help of someone from the FBI office."

"Well, I have more interesting news for you."

"What's that?"

"You remember how you asked me to look up the DA," Brognola asked.

"Yeah?"

"I found him. Rather I should say I found him and his family. The bodies were stuffed inside barrels and thrown into the Gulf. They washed up on shore in Alabama. They probably sank initially, but during decomp the gases brought them back up. So far we have the DA and his wife, our expectation is to find his daughter, as well."

There was a long pause as Bolan contemplated the evil

that it took to kill a whole family in cold blood. There was bad in the world, and then there was true evil.

"Look, Striker, I know you won't leave, but it's past time for me to send in a team. You could use the backup, it sounds like, at least until the smoke clears and we can figure out who the real players are in this thing."

"Send them in, Hal," he said. "And they can pick up whatever pieces are left when they get here, but I saw Rio alive and I'm getting him out."

"I'm sending a team," the big Fed said. "I'll have them contact you as soon as they arrive."

Bolan hung up the sat phone and opened another drawer. From inside, he removed an advanced surveillance kit, then he turned to Remy. "Time to go," he said. "We're going to find out what's really going on around here."

16

The thick trees and endless turns would make escape impossible to anyone who didn't understand their surroundings, but with Remy's intimate knowledge of the bayou, Bolan guided the big SUV to a nearly invisible path that ran parallel to Nick Costello's compound. The makeshift road stopped at a cemetery that might have had use back during the Civil War. The few headstones left standing were moss-covered or had fallen onto their sides, and many of the graves were unmarked. Oddly, there was one headstone that was standing up properly, cleaned, and had flowers on it that were no more than a few days old. It didn't appear to be quite as old as the others in the plot, which wasn't very large, but it was the only one in decent condition.

"One of yours?" Bolan asked Remy, pointing at the grave. From his angle, he couldn't read the name.

"Nope," he said, "but every time I've passed this way that one is taken care of." Remy shrugged. "It's kind of creepy to tell you the truth."

"One of those New Orleans ghost stories," Bolan said, moving to the back of the SUV once more.

"Costello's compound is about a mile or so from here," Remy said, joining him. "But the terrain isn't too bad if we need to get closer."

Bolan shook his head. "No, this should do it. It's got a pretty decent range, so if I can lock in on a signal, we should be good to go." He began setting up the equipment in the open tailgate, moving the trio of parabolic dishes in opposite directions, one aimed toward the southern coast, and the other toward Costello's compound. The third was pointed almost straight up.

"The Border Patrol and the Coast Guard have listening towers all along the coast," he said. "This little toy will ping a satellite in low orbit and use the listening towers to give a boost to the receiver. You have to know the exact coordinates, but it works surprisingly well."

"We never had one of those in the SEALs," Remy said. "And I can think of a few times it would've come in handy."

"Give it another couple of years and they'll show up," he said. "I sometimes have access to state-of-the-art gadgets." He tapped several keys on the console of the device, inputting coordinates for the satellite, and then making adjustments for the listening towers. "This won't work very far inland, but on most of the borders, you've got a pretty good shot at it.

"And that," Bolan said as he engaged the uplink, "should be just about it." He handed Remy a headset and put on his own. After listening for a moment, he adjusted the receiver frequency, and after several tries, he started hearing voices from inside the compound. Initially, the conversations were random, mostly perimeter guards, but then after several more adjustments, he heard a voice he recognized and gave Remy a thumbs-up.

"Perotti is here to see you, boss." The first voice was Salerno's.

"Perotti, huh? What a surprise."

That had to have been Costello's voice, and Bolan made a

mental note to think carefully about it later. Something about his accent bothered him.

"Send him in."

"Perotti, you dumb bastard! What the hell is going on? Our arrangement was that I handle the locals and you were going to deal with the Feds. Now I hear you've got a dead FBI agent on your hands. Don't I have enough to do without worry about your end of things?"

"I can handle the Feds. And Lacroix has already been released on his own recognizance. By the time the mess at the DA's office gets straightened out, there won't be any evidence to pursue the case. Grady was depressed, you know. Looks like suicide."

"Good. What else you got for me?"

"You already know that Remy Fountainou and this guy Cooper are still on the loose. I practically handed them to you, and they slipped right through your fingers."

"My fingers? I notice they also got out of your ambush at the church."

"They aren't going to be easy to nab. I pulled the files on both of them before I came out here."

"And?"

"Fountainou is an ex-Navy SEAL, highly decorated. And I don't know who this Cooper character really is. He claimed to be a U.S. marshal, but his file didn't even start until he was supposedly assigned to the Jack Rio case, which means it's a cover of some kind. Maybe he's Special Forces or something."

"Or something. We need both of them dead and gone."

"I've got warrants out on them both, but once they're arrested and in custody, it won't take long for someone to figure out that something isn't right. It would be better if they died resisting arrest or simply disappeared."

"Then you handle it, for Christ's sake! I've got to get these weapons in and out of my warehouse. I've been told that the Israelis are aware of the thefts from their transport ships, and they've already got people combing the docks and the coast looking for their stuff."

"Then you better get what you need from that agent fast. You'll need those routes into Mexico if you're going to get everything to your buyers. Plus, with all of the fuss here we'll be able to use the route to get more weapons in. I have some people that are very interested in getting other things into the U.S., but only if we can show them some prior successes."

"Then take care of Remy and Cooper, damn it!"

"I'll try, but you'd best have your men on full alert and combing the streets. I have to get back to the FBI office in town."

Bolan had heard enough. He slipped off his headphones and looked at Remy.

"That son of a bitch killed his own man!" the ex-SEAL snapped.

"Yeah, it sounds like he did. How about you and I go and have a visit with him? We can discuss the oath he took and remind him what the penalty for treason is. Besides, he owes me a flash drive."

AFTER PACKING UP the surveillance gear, Bolan and Remy headed back into the city and managed to pick up Perotti's car just before the traffic got heavy. His blue BMW wasn't hard to miss, and he drove as if he didn't have a care in the world, stopping for coffee before heading into work. They followed him back to the FBI offices and waited for him to enter the building.

"How are we going to get in there?" Remy asked. "I've heard they keep the building pretty secure."

"They do," Bolan replied, "but most every lock has a key." He pulled out his sat phone and linked it to the in-dash GPS screen, then dialed a number from memory, mentally thanking Akira Tokaido for the "hacking" lessons. After a series of tones, he punched in another code and the in-dash screen flickered and showed a menu.

"How the hell did you do that?" Remy asked.

"That's a phone-based hack into the FBI administrative server," he replied. "It's not as secure as the personnel files, and it's practically an open door compared to the case files." He selected the icon labeled MAINTENANCE, and this opened a number of folders with labels ranging from GROUNDS/JANITORIAL to HVAC. The one he wanted was labeled SCHEMATICS.

Bolan selected that one and then found the one for the New Orleans office and opened it. Remy whistled softly as a detailed floor plan came up on the screen. Bolan studied it for a minute, then pointed to a rear set of doors near the loading dock. "We'll go in there," he said.

"Won't they be locked?" Remy asked.

Bolan nodded. "But I'm pretty sure I can get us in anyway. Once we're inside, we'll use the stairs—the elevators are pass card protected—and then go to Perotti's office."

They exited the SUV, locked it and walked around the block to the alley that led to the back of the building. "It's not likely that there will be guards," Bolan said quietly. "But there will definitely be security cameras, so we'll need to move quickly."

"Understood," he said.

They reached the edge of the building, and Bolan scanned the back wall. "I think our best approach is to act like we belong," he said. "So long as my way in works, we shouldn't have any trouble."

"I'll follow your lead," Remy said.

Bolan moved quickly down the alley, with Remy hot on his heels, and made it to the back door. The loading dock entrance was shut and locked tight, while the main rear entry doors had a single light burning above them. There was a magnetic lock on the door that used a card reader. Bolan pulled out the key card from his wallet and slid it through the reader.

"Here's where it gets tricky," he said. The pad beeped once and a small LED display appeared saying: PASSCODE.

Bolan keyed in the janitorial override code he'd seen on the building schematic in the database. The pad beeped a second time, flashed the word CLEAR and then unlocked.

The soldier opened it and stepped inside, gesturing for Remy to follow him.

"You seem to get all the best toys," the big man said quietly. "Who do you work for, really?"

"If we live through this, I'll see what I can do to get you an introduction," he replied. "They're always looking for a few good men with your kind of experience."

"Good to know," Remy said.

The offices were closed for the night, and they used the service stairwell to reach the upper floor where Bolan figured Perotti's office to be. It was an odd thing, but virtually every FBI office had the same layout, with the most powerful man commanding the biggest office at the top. It made them predictable, but it served his purposes.

He moved into the floor and saw that light spilled from the corner office. "That's where he'll be," Bolan whispered, then moved out down the hall.

As they reached the office, Remy rushed past the soldier, hitting Perotti's door at a near dead run. Bolan moved in behind him in time to watch as Remy snagged Perotti by the throat, yanking him up and out of his chair, then slamming him forcefully onto the top of the desk.

There was a stunned, wild-eyed look on the FBI agent's

face as the giant ex-SEAL towered over him. "Don't kill him yet Remy. I still need some information."

It took a few seconds for the words to penetrate the rage that Remy was in. His strong muscles flexed, veins popping as the tension filled him. Bolan knew that the man could snap Perotti's neck at any moment, but even in his rage he was still trying to do the right thing. Bolan watched the wave of emotions washing over Remy and just waited. The man had strong feelings about someone who would subvert not only federal law enforcement, but would also kill one of his own agents to do it.

Remy took a deep, calming breath, then slowly eased up on Perotti's throat. "Ask your questions," he said.

Bolan stared down at the man responsible for Agent Grady Black's death and felt his own anger flow through him. "I want the drive that you took from Grady when you killed him," he said.

"I don't know what you're talking about," Perotti rasped. "Agent Black's out on a case."

Bolan drew his Desert Eagle, worked the slide and brought it to bear on the agent's temple. "I've already got you on surveillance talking to Costello about Agent Black's so-called suicide."

"How did you… You're bluffing," Perotti said.

"Not really. We heard everything and have it all recorded. This evidence won't conveniently disappear. Justice will be served," Bolan replied. "But shooting's too good for you. Remy, if the next words out of his mouth aren't helpful, I want you to rip off one of his arms."

Remy grasped the man's arm and twisted it. "Should come right off when I give it a good yank," he said. "Shoulder joints are weak."

Perotti looked from one man to the other. He reached down to open his desk drawer. Remy snatched his hand.

"The drive is in my drawer," Perotti said.

"Open it slowly," Bolan told him.

Perotti opened the drawer, pulled out the drive and handed it to him. "Get him out of the way," Bolan said, and Remy yanked the man to his feet and shoved him into a chair beside the desk.

Perotti's computer was already up and running, so Bolan didn't have to ask for any passwords or logins. He put the drive into an open USB port and waited for it to read. When it did, he saw that it contained only music files. He looked once at Remy and shook his head.

Remy threw a hard punch to Perotti's middle, doubling him over. Bolan wondered if Perotti felt that all the way to his spine.

"We already have you cold," Bolan told him. "You're not getting away, and when I'm done, neither will anyone else in Mr. Costello's payroll. I'm going to ask again. Where is the drive?"

"It was a mistake," Perotti babbled. "They all look the same! Look in my drawer, there's another there."

Bolan pulled open the drawer and removed another flash drive. He popped it into the computer's USB port and pulled up the files. It was the genuine article. He opened a browser window and navigated to a secure site, then logged into a Web account through a virtual server and transferred the files from the drive. Once it was complete, he logged out, and called Hal Brognola.

"Hal, I got the files," he said. "I've already sent them your way through back channels. It'll take a minute."

Moments later there was the faint sound of a clicking keyboard, then the big Fed said, "Good job, Striker. Do you still have Perotti?"

"Yeah."

"Find out what he did with Grady's body. I want to try to give him a proper burial."

"I'll see what I can do," Bolan said. "Is the team en route?"

"Yes, and I've got word into the U.S. Marshal Service office down there as well. They're standing by, just waiting to hear from you. They've agreed not to ask questions about who you work for."

"Good," Bolan said, then hung up Perotti's phone and looked through the files in the desk. He grabbed what he thought he would need and turned back to the agent.

"If you have anything to tell us before I decide what to do with you, this might be your last chance to save your skin."

"If you want a trial, you don't want to touch me. As it is, you're in violation of my civil rights and about a dozen law-enforcement codes. I don't have anything to tell you."

"So you don't want to discuss what the hell you were doing at Costello's compound talking about the murder of Agent Black and your treason?" Bolan asked.

"Go to hell Cooper. What do you really know about anything?"

"I know that at some point in your life your oath had to mean something. I know that betraying a comrade in arms comes at a price. Why don't you try to do one last good thing? Something that is worthy of that badge you've been toting around."

Perotti paused and looked at Bolan. His once pressed and polished appearance was a thing of the past, replaced by sweat-soaked clothes. Bolan watched the man's eyes for some sense of remorse or contrition, but the only emotion present was hatred.

"I made my deal a long time ago, Cooper, and so did you. Don't feign innocence with me for one minute. I know what you're capable of."

Bolan shook his head. He knew that there were some lines you couldn't uncross. He looked up at Remy.

"It's your choice. What do you want to do with him? We can just handcuff him and turn him in to the marshals."

Remy considered it for a minute, then looked at Perotti. "He deserves to die, but he should stand trial for his crimes. I want everyone to know how he betrayed his country and his oath."

The Executioner nodded and made the call to the marshals' office. Then he tucked the files under his arm and started to walk to the door.

"Marshals are on their way to take you into custody," Bolan told Perotti. "We'll hand you over to them, which is more than you deserve."

Perotti laughed, almost maniacally. "You think you've got me, Cooper? None of this will ever see the light of day. I might lose my badge, but I'll be on the street in less than six months. And when that day comes, I'll be looking for you. I'll find you, Cooper, and I'll kill you." He laughed again. "Assuming Costello doesn't get you first."

The Executioner was going to say something, but then noticed Perotti's left hand reaching for something under the desk. Bolan pulled the Desert Eagle in one smooth motion, turned and shot him in the heart. The report echoed in the small office as Perotti slumped back into the chair, dead. The 9 mm pistol that he'd grabbed dropped to the floor.

"I guess I should have handcuffed him. Too bad he won't be able to stand trial," Remy said.

"He just testified," Bolan said quietly. "And I was judge, jury and executioner."

17

Bolan and Remy knew the resonating sound of the gunshot would bring security on the double, so they left the office running and hit the stairwell at full speed. Fortune smiled on them, and they got out of the building without incident. Once outside, they quickly returned to the SUV. Bolan handed the file he'd taken to Remy, who began to flip through it while they drove through the city.

Remy suggested they could lie low for a time at a blues club, right on the edge of the French Quarter, and Bolan agreed. By the time they got there, the club was shutting down for the night, but the owner was a friend of Remy's and waved them in. The Spotted Cat was in a tiny two-story building tucked between two towering office buildings. The interior was bricked along the stage wall, with stools lined up for the acts to use. Bolan looked around as Remy spoke with the owner. The memorabilia that lined the walls would have made any music lover envious. A whispered conversation between the two men resulted in the owner quickly locking up and heading to his apartment upstairs, after telling them to take all the time they needed.

Remy walked behind the bar and poured himself a Red Horse beer from the tap. He held a second large glass mug up to Bolan. "Want one?" he asked.

"No, thanks," he said. "But is that coffee behind you warm?"

Remy put a hand on the side of the pot. "Yeah, but I got no idea how old it is. You might be drinking Mississippi mud."

"It'll be fine," he said. "This is the first place that I've seen in New Orleans that makes me appreciate the city. We'll get rid of some of the thugs, and maybe people can enjoy the music and the history again."

Remy poured Bolan a mug of the black coffee and brought it to a table along with his beer. They settled down with the files Bolan had taken from Perotti's office, and began sifting through the pages.

Bolan couldn't believe that Perotti had been corrupt for so many years, long before Costello was added to the mix. He had been using the international ports and waterways as his own personal loan shark and shipping empire. His bank records showed accounts in the Caymans, Switzerland and Argentina.

"Hey, look at this," Remy said, holding out another sheet of paper for Bolan's inspection. "This is interesting."

He added the sheet to the pages he was already compiling, all of which were related to shipments of Israeli weapons. But the crates Bolan had seen in the warehouse were small potatoes compared to the list in front of him. In the warehouse, he'd only noticed assault rifles and small arms, but this list included antitank missiles, explosives and communications gear designed to pick up on satellite transmissions. These weren't just arms to be supplied to private security forces, these were the kinds of munitions that could start wars in certain parts of the world.

"It looks like they were pulling stuff straight off the ships in the Gulf," Bolan said. "Some of these lists are stamped like a manifest."

"They're getting into some pretty serious weapons here,"

Remy said. "Assault rifles are bad enough, but one of these antitank weapons could take out a small building. I also see some higher yield explosives that might have an interesting impact, like say blowing a hole in the side of a building. This would be pretty big stuff on the black market."

"I've got an idea," Bolan said suddenly.

"What's that?" Remy asked.

"That I haven't talked to the right people yet," he replied. Bolan picked up his cell phone and hit the auto-dial for Brognola.

"What have you got?" Brognola said as he picked up.

"I need you to use one of your contacts. I've got a hunch."

THE PHONE RANG twice before a heavily accented voice answered. "Amit," Bolan said, "I'm sorry to call so late, but I'm a colleague of Hal Brognola and he said you might be able to help me out with a very urgent matter." Amit was an Israeli intelligence officer stationed at the embassy in Washington, D.C.

"Men in our business are not allowed the luxury of uninterrupted rest, my friend. What can I do for you?"

"Do you have a secure fax line?" Bolan asked.

"Of course," Amit said, rattling off the number.

"One second," Bolan said, turning to Remy. "Does your friend own a fax machine?" When Remy nodded in the affirmative, Bolan handed him the sheaf of papers and gave him the number. "Send this over for me, would you?"

Remy took the papers and headed toward the small office behind the bar.

"I have a file of information that I'm going to send you," Bolan told Amit. "It should be coming through in just a minute."

Amit asked for him to hold while he transferred the call,

and picked it back up several minutes later. "The pages are coming through now," he said.

"Good." Bolan then filled Amit in on Costello, Perotti and Lacroix. "From what I can tell, they're stealing this stuff right off your transport ships. Are you getting reports of missing hardware?" He could hear the sound of papers being shuffled in the background.

"Yes, actually," Amit said. "We've got investigators working the area now. We had three shipments come up short, but we weren't certain where the theft was happening in the supply chain. We caught it earlier on the last shipment, so we've been having the vessels stay anchored in the same area while it is being investigated. Some of the things that were taken are…sensitive."

"Looking at the list, I can see why they would be a cause for concern. I'm glad you're holding the ships. Maybe if we work together we can figure out which parties may be involved," he said.

"Do you have any photographs of these men?" Amit asked.

Bolan looked through the papers on the table and found color copies of identification. "Yeah," he said. "I've got them."

"Can you send them to me?"

"Sure, hold on a moment," Bolan said. He used his phone to take a picture of each one up close, then sent them to Amit via email. "On the way."

"My personal email?" he asked.

"Yes. Hal supplied me with your address," Bolan replied.

"One moment, then," Amit said. "Stand by."

Bolan held for a couple of moments, then the intelligence officer came back on the line. "Are you sure the names are all correct?" he asked.

"As far as I know," he said. "Why?"

"Because the man in the picture identified as Nick Costello is not him."

"I don't understand," he said.

"This man is not real Mafia," Amit said. "He's not even Italian."

"You're kidding," Bolan replied. "Then who is he?"

"A man we tracked for several years, then we lost him. His name is Nikolai Agron, and he's old Russian KGB. Back when it all started to fall apart, he was selling off parts of the Russian war machine before anyone else had even considered it. His greed got him chased out of Russia, and he turned up in several other places using different names, but around 2005, he vanished. In truth, we assumed he was dead."

Several lights went on in Bolan's mind, including why Costello's accent seemed funny to him. He was very good at disguising it, but the hint was there for an experienced listener. "Damn, that explains a lot," he said. "For one thing, so far as I can tell, he rarely leaves his compound."

"With your permission, I would like to share this information with one of my compatriots in Russian intelligence. He would be very happy if I could give him Agron's location, and it would clear up a debt between us."

"You can tell him, Amit, but I wouldn't count on them getting to him before I do."

"I do not suppose you would consider waiting," he said, his voice expressing dismay. "At least for some of my people? This series of thefts is being taken very seriously by many in the upper ranks, and it's one of our top priorities at the moment. There is a lot of pride that needs to be soothed."

"I'm sorry, but all of this is coming to a head and I'm going to finish it. Still, you should probably have someone in the area who can verify that the weapons belong to you, and I'd appreciate anything you've got on Agron. I'd like to know who I'm really dealing with here."

"The file is no trouble, and I can have someone from the embassy down there as soon as possible…" Amit's voice trailed off for a moment, then he said, "But do not be surprised if others are on their way, as well."

"Just tell your people two men out there are on their side," Bolan said. "I don't want to be caught in a cross fire."

"Of course," he said. "Thank you for coming to me with this. I want this stopped. My government will be extremely grateful, and it will probably mean a promotion."

"And thanks for your help," Bolan said, then hung up the phone. Remy had returned to the table and finished his beer. The soldier related the conversation he'd just had, and finished just as the file on Agron came through to his phone.

He opened the file and he and Remy looked at it together.

"Ex-KGB, all kinds of trafficking, including drugs, weapons and even women into the sex-slave trade in Eastern Europe. An all around class act," Bolan finished sarcastically.

"So he's not even Italian," Remy said. "You know, I bet some of the people working for him might look down on that kind of thing."

Bolan opened his phone and dialed again. Maybe lighting a fire under the real Mafia would help their odds.

The voice on the other end sounded extremely unhappy. "Who the fuck is this, and why are you calling me in the middle of the night?"

"Is this Angelo Cosenza of Chicago?"

"Yeah, it is. Who the hell are you?"

"Let's just say I'm a concerned citizen just calling to give you some information."

"Why the hell would you do that?" he said.

Bolan didn't respond, just relayed the story of how Nick

Costello, posing as a mafioso in New Orleans, was actually a Russian thug named Nikolai Agron.

"The hell you say," Angelo said. "If this is true, he's got some balls on him."

"Big ones," Bolan agreed. "Just thought you'd want to know."

"I'll take care of it—and him—personally," Cosenza said.

"Better hurry," he replied. "I think this guy has a lot of trouble coming his way."

There was a long pause, followed by an odd, rasping sound that he quickly realized was laughter. Finally Cosenza said, "Yeah, you got that right," and he hung up the phone.

Bolan gathered up the papers on the table and finished his coffee, while Remy drank the last of his beer.

"I have a thought," Remy said, "if you want to hear it."

"Go ahead," he said.

"I don't know what everyone you've called will do, but if they thin the herd, I'm liking our odds a little better."

"Real mafiosi hate impostors," Bolan replied. "Especially ones who are taking money out of their hands and putting it into their own pockets. They'll take it personally."

"And the Israelis?"

"For them, it will be a matter of national security and public pride. If Costello gets those weapons into the hands of his buyer, the trail will ultimately lead back to the Israelis. It would be a big mess and a public relations nightmare for them. They'll act quickly, and the Russians will be right behind them."

"Then we better move fast, because it sounds like you're going to have more guns on your side than he does."

"Costello is a bonus," Bolan said. "More importantly, I

want to get Rio out alive. That's why I came here in the first place."

Remy took his empty glass and Bolan's mug to the bar. "Then let's get moving."

"IT'S ALL FALLING APART," Nick said. "We're out of time."

"What's happened?" Victor Salerno asked.

"Perotti is dead, killed in his own office, and it looks like a bunch of his files are apparently missing."

"That's bad," he agreed.

"It gets worse. The docks are awash with Israelis on 'shore leave,' and even a few Russians."

"Russians? Why?" Salerno asked.

"Who the hell knows?" Nick said, but of course he did. His cover had somehow been completely blown. It was only a matter of time until the real Italian Mafia got involved as well, and when Salerno found out that he wasn't who he said he was… He shook his head. "Put an extra guard on Rio, and move him to a secure room in the center of the house. I want the gates closed and the perimeter sealed. No one in or out without my permission."

"Okay, Nick," he said.

"This guy Cooper… This has to be it with this guy. He's coming, I can feel it. We need to end this and get our weapons out. Things will calm down then."

"What about Rio?"

"I'm going to finish with the marshal next. If he doesn't give me what we need, then I'll whack him and we'll do it the hard way."

"Trucks overland?" Salerno asked.

"Yeah," he said. "The Israelis are going to be heading our way soon, so we need this done."

"I'll take care of Cooper and his friend, boss," Salerno said. "Just get those routes."

"I'll do my part, you just do yours. Take care of this nut— and good. I don't want to be looking over my shoulder."

18

Bolan watched Costello's compound through his binoculars. It was a pretty good setup, he had to admit. There were at least twenty-five men patrolling the grounds, and all of them were armed with Israeli assault rifles, mostly Tavor TAR-21s. The majority of the men paced the perimeter, while four guarded the main gate, which was closed and locked. The main house resembled an embassy, two floors with secure exits and probably a lower level for storage.

"How do you want to play this?" Remy asked.

"He's gone into lockdown, which means he's aware of at least some of the trouble headed his way," Bolan said. "If we don't take him now, it's going to get crowded." He looked over the compound once more. "I'm going to need a distraction on the perimeter big enough to open a hole for me to go through, then I want you to play God."

Remy scanned the area, then pointed. "There's a stand of trees over there that looks sturdy enough," he said. "Good cover and position."

"That works," Bolan said. "I'm going in just to the right of the main gate. The wall is a little lower there, and it's the shortest route to the house."

"We can set up charges on the wall there," Remy said, pointing again, "and there. Once we're both in position, we can set them off. That should pull most of the guards away from your entry point, and then I can watch your six through the scope."

"My objective at this point is to get Rio out," Bolan said. "I'll deal with Costello or whatever his real name is after I take care of the marshal." He checked the grounds through the binoculars once more and spotted an all-too-familiar figure.

"That guy," Bolan said, pointing, "Victor Salerno. He's Costello's capo. If we can get him, that will be a nice bonus. I don't think Costello will be able to keep pulling men to him without Salerno."

"Perhaps we'll get lucky then," he said.

They returned to the SUV to finish gearing up, which included putting on wireless headsets that would let them stay in contact throughout the assault. Bolan prepped two small blocks of C-4 with a timer and detonator and put them in his bag. Remy slid the M-16 A-4 from its case. It had a small scope and a laser sight that would serve his needs very well, but more important was the sound suppressor attached to the end of the barrel. He took several magazines for the rifle, as well as a couple for his .45. A small grappling hook attached to a rappelling line, along with both Desert Eagles and ammunition, completed Bolan's equipment.

"You set the charges," Remy said, "then move into position. That should give you plenty of time to get around to the gate while I hightail it into the trees." He moved off toward the back side of the compound, while Bolan headed for the front.

The Executioner moved along the outer perimeter and placed the first charge on the stone wall and set the timer. He moved down the wall and pulled the second charge from his bag.

Bolan heard the rustle of leaves a split second before

the guard was on top of him. The guard tackled him to the ground. Bolan twisted to one side and brought his elbow back into the guy's face. The guard loosened his hold enough that the soldier could wedge his knee underneath himself and roll the two of them over. Two short jabs to the face and the sentry stopped fighting.

As Bolan started to back off, the guard pulled a knife and tried to stab him in the side. The soldier grabbed his hand and turned the knife toward his adversary. The strength contest had begun, but Bolan knew he needed to get out of there quickly. One burst with all of his body weight had the knife lodged in the guy's throat.

He finished setting the charge and double-timed it back to his position. Once he reached a good vantage point, he said, "I'm in position. Ready when you are. Ninety seconds."

"Copy that," Remy answered.

Bolan watched the seconds count down and the C-4 went off with a thunderous boom. From where he was positioned, he could see the rock wall shatter and smoke fill the air. The blast set off the alarm system as well, a high warbling siren that would make it difficult for Costello's crew to communicate with one another. Men were running toward the explosion from every direction.

Bolan swung the line and tossed the grapple, the pitons catching the lip of the wall. He tugged, then climbed quickly, reaching the top and scanned the gate area for any remaining guards. His eyes found one holdout, but before he could draw and fire, a red wound opened on the man's chest, and he fell over dead.

"God is still watching," Remy said.

Bolan tossed the line over the other side and descended into the main courtyard. With no time to waste, he headed for the house. As two more of the guards near the explosion site went down, some of Costello's men began firing randomly into the swamp, while several others tried to bring order to the chaos.

The erupting of the second charge, ten feet farther along the wall, caught them by surprise. Six men went down in the blast, either from the concussion or the pieces of rock flying through the air. Bolan gained the courtyard between the main house and the bunkhouse.

"Hey, you!"

Bolan turned as a sentry appeared from the trees along the front of the house, only a few yards away. Hoping to keep his presence inside the compound unnoticed, the Executioner turned toward the man, the combat knife a blur in his hand as he threw it.

The blade buried itself in the sentry's throat. Bolan kept moving toward him, catching the guy as he fell. The soldier pulled the knife free of the corpse, wiped the blade on the guy's shirt and replaced it in its scabbard. Then he dragged the body back into the trees.

Bolan moved to the bunkhouse. He ran along the wall in a crouch, keeping out of sight of the windows. As he began to round a corner, a shot splintered the wood above his head. He ducked back. More shots started coming from the windows as yelling people gave away his position. Bolan pulled a grenade from the pouch at his waist, armed it and tossed the bomb on the roof of the bunkhouse. The explosion rocked the ground and tore the roof as if it were tissue paper, sending roofing materials and wood tumbling to the ground. Bolan tried the corner only to be stymied by shots again. Someone had him pegged.

"I got it," Remy said over the com-link.

Although he couldn't hear the shot, a second later Bolan picked up a faint thud as a body dropped to the ground. He got on the move again, running to the back side of the main house. Three men stood guard at the door. The soldier drew the Desert Eagle and fired, hitting the first two. The third man turned to run, causing him to miss, but by then, the Executioner was almost on top of him. Bolan reholstered on the run, caught the man and snapped his neck.

He reached the door, opened it and saw that the room was a kitchen. He stepped inside, and almost immediately two shots rang out, forcing him to duck. Bolan reached out and opened the refrigerator door, glad for its stainless-steel protection.

"You're a pain in the ass, Cooper," Salerno called. "You're supposed to be dead."

"You'd be surprised how often I've heard that," Bolan replied. "Usually right before I kill someone."

Bolan fired two quick shots around the refrigerator door. The sound was immense in the small, tiled space of the kitchen. Salerno didn't reply, but dropped beneath the bullets, slamming into the refrigerator door with his feet. Bolan skidded backward, lost his balance, fell and rolled, losing the Desert Eagle in the process. He came up on his feet and followed through with a spinning roundhouse kick to Salerno's head.

The thug took the kick on the shoulder and bulled ahead, trying for the head-butt. Bolan stepped back, then lunged forward again with two stiff jabs to Salerno's face.

A look of disbelief passed across his features as the blood started to run, and Salerno realized he was seriously overmatched. The man backed away and turned to take off, then stopped and grabbed a chair with his good arm, swinging it wildly.

Bolan dodged low, dropped his shoulders and charged, knocking the big Italian to the ground. He went to move in, but one of Salerno's men pulled him off, spun him and swung for his face. The soldier blocked, head butted the man and kneed him in the gut, then followed with a knife-hand blow to the back of the neck. The man went down, unconscious.

The Executioner turned back to just in time to see the knife that Salerno was going to stab into his back. He captured Salerno's wrist, pulled him in and brought the heel of his hand across his elbow. The joint snapped like a heavy branch, and Salerno howled in pain as he dropped the knife.

"Where's Rio?" Bolan asked, applying pressure to the break.

"Upstairs," Salerno said through gritted teeth, "but you'll never get to him in time. Costello's been up there already this morning. He'll have had a little more fun and then killed him."

Bolan balled up his meaty fist and planted in the center of Salerno's face. Blood spurted from the broken nose. He went down, and the soldier started to walk away, stopping when he saw Salerno drag a gun free of a holster with his already damaged arm.

The mafioso tried to lift it, but his shoulder wouldn't cooperate and the shot went wild. "Where the hell do you think you're going?" he shouted.

"You're dead already," Bolan said. "You just don't know it yet. You're not worth the bullet."

Salerno fired again, shattering a window. "*You're* the dead man, Cooper," he grated.

"Salerno," Bolan said, "the man you're working for isn't even Italian. He's a Russian named Nikolai Agron. You think the real Mob is going to allow any of you to live after this?"

Salerno raised the gun a final time, but before he could pull the trigger, a shot rang out from the doorway, knocking him back to the floor, dead at last.

Bolan looked and saw Remy standing there. "You didn't think I was going to let you have all the fun, did you?"

"I suppose not," he said.

"Besides, God couldn't see into the house," Remy said. "I've got your back, so let's go."

DESPITE TAKING every precaution, it was over. From the balcony on the second floor, Nick—Nikolai—watched as the perimeter came apart, a sniper somewhere in the trees taking out his guards one by one, as someone else blew up the bunkhouse. A few minutes later, shots rang out on the lower level of the building. All this chaos, plus he had failed to get what he needed from the U.S. marshal. It was time to go.

He went back inside, grabbed his emergency bag, opened a panel and took a set of hidden stairs down to the first floor, then a passageway that led to the front of the house. As more shots came from the kitchen, Nick slipped through the front door and across the porch to where his truck was waiting for him. All hell might have broken loose, but if he—Nikolai—was an expert in anything, disappearing was at the top of the list.

The few remaining guards were already running away—or in most cases, he thought, slinking away like cowards. Nick spotted one trying to take cover near the rear of his truck. He pulled out his 9 mm pistol and shot the man. Several others stopped in their tracks.

"Get your asses in there," he said, gesturing with the gun, "and take care of this problem." He pointed the weapon at them. "Or I'll kill you myself."

The men looked at the gun that was trained on them and started to head back toward the house. He had no hope that it would do more than delay Cooper and Remy, but that was all he needed. Time to get away.

Nick climbed into the driver's seat, started the engine and took off for the docks.

19

Bolan picked up the Tavor assault rifle dropped by Salerno's man along with a couple of extra magazines, then he and Remy ran into the main part of the house, crossing into the living room. They immediately began taking fire from men stationed in the foyer. They ducked behind a thick sofa that offered some cover as bullets drilled into the room.

"How many?" Remy asked.

"Four, I think," Bolan said, signaling left for himself. "Maybe a couple more."

A brief lull in the firing came and both men jumped up, using the back of the couch like a row of sandbags. Bolan cut loose with the Tavor in sharp 3-round bursts, and was rewarded with a high, warbling screech as one of the attackers took a round in the leg. He stumbled from behind the pillar he was using as cover, and Remy finished him off with his .45.

"Noisy bastard," he muttered.

When their magazines cycled dry, they took shelter behind the couch again, and another hail of gunfire poured into the room. Both men reloaded. "Let's finish it," Bolan said as they went topside again.

He quickly took out two more men on the left, the Tavor spitting rounds with smooth, precise action. Remy fired several times, forcing a man on the stairs to run for better cover, then shot him when he hit the bottom step.

One final man popped out of a coat closet and tried making a run for it, but went down as both Bolan and Remy opened fire. Quiet descended once more, and the pair reloaded as they moved into the foyer, keeping their eyes open for trouble.

They saw a few more of Costello's men, but all of them were trying to escape, not fight, which told Bolan that Costello had already fled the scene. With Salerno dead, and the moneyman disappearing, most of these men would be far better at running than fighting.

Remy and Bolan mounted the stairs to the second floor, and after a short fight with two men who were ransacking an office, Bolan burst through a door to see Rio bound to a chair and gagged with a sock of some kind.

His eyes were bulging wide and he was desperately trying to say something, but the warning came too late. One of Costello's last remaining holdouts stepped from behind a curtain covering the balcony, firing a 9 mm pistol as fast as he could pull the trigger. Remy took a round in the left shoulder that would have probably knocked down a smaller man. As it was, he spun sideways, his own return shot going wide.

The Executioner fired the Tavor from hip level, squeezing off several quick rounds that punched into the man's chest and forced him back through the curtain and outside onto the balcony. Bolan stepped forward and fired twice more and the guy went over the rail, dead before he hit the ground.

"You all right?" Bolan asked, turning back to Remy.

"I'll live," he said, heading for the bathroom. "Check Rio."

Bolan moved to Rio and used his knife to cut the ropes that held him to the chair. Badly bruised and beaten, Rio sagged forward into Bolan's arms. Blood seeped from wounds on his legs. Bolan reached up to check the man's pulse. It was rapid and thready, which meant the marshal was already dehydrated. Guessing from the amount of blood on him, Rio would need a transfusion.

"Hey, you must be the cavalry," he whispered, "but what took you so long?"

Bolan lowered him to the floor and said softly, "Well, the next time you get kidnapped, try to pick a situation that's a little less complicated. The name's Cooper—sent on behalf of your brother." He pulled two heavy trauma bandages out of the bag at his waist and applied one to Rio's knee and the other around his thigh. Tying them off with quick knots caused the marshal to grimace in renewed pain.

The soldier reached into the small medic kit and grabbed a shot of morphine, holding it up for Rio to see. "No time to argue with me. We need to get you out of here and the less pain you're in, the easier it'll be to move you. A lot of men are running, but there are still a few holdouts firing in our direction."

Rio laughed weakly. "No arguments, Cooper. After days of fun in the game room, I'll take whatever you can give me."

Bolan shot the needle into Rio's thigh. "That should kick in pretty fast," he said. "Just rest for a minute, then we'll go." He turned his attention to Remy.

From the bathroom, the big man had grabbed a heavy cotton towel and was holding it to his shoulder, but it had already soaked through in a couple of places. "I need to look at that wound," Bolan said, pulling the towel away. It wasn't too bad, but it was bleeding pretty freely, and there wasn't an exit wound.

"Looks like it's buried somewhere behind your collarbone," Bolan said. "We need to get the bleeding stopped, but it's going to have to wait." He pulled the last trauma bandage out of his kit and applied it to the wound, tying it off as tightly as he could. "You okay?"

Though he could tell that Remy had paled a bit, the big man nodded gamely. "I'll grab another towel while you get Rio on his feet." He went back into the bathroom and Bolan returned to where Rio was stretched out on the floor.

"Time to go," he said, slipping an arm underneath the man's shoulders. "Ready?"

Rio nodded, his pupils dilated with the effect of the morphine.

Bolan got him upright just as Remy returned with another towel, this one torn into strips. "Let's go," he said.

They went out the door and down the hall to the stairs and started down when more gunshots rang out below them and outside. Pulling back, Bolan muttered, "I thought they were all dead or gone."

"Me, too," Remy said.

Bolan peered down the stairs and into the foyer, while Remy helped keep Rio on his feet. "Hang on," he said, moving into position by a large potted plant.

The front doors were open and several men were milling around just inside, reloading. Bolan checked the last clip he had in the Tavor and decided it would have to do. Switching it to full-auto, he launched himself down the stairs, firing as he went.

Three men went down before the magazine was emptied, and he drew the Desert Eagle as he got to the bottom. Bullets filled the air, but they were panic shots, while Bolan's were expertly placed. He took two more men down, then ducked behind a pillar.

Outside, the sound of helicopter blades announced the arrival of backup, and the last of Costello's men raced outside, trying to get away. Bolan reloaded, then ran back up the stairs to where Remy and Rio were still waiting. "Let's move out," he said.

They made it down the steps and out onto the porch as a pair of choppers landed in the courtyard and two teams clad in black fatigues and bristling with weapons jumped out to secure the immediate area. Bolan recognized one of the pilots as Charlie Mott. "These are the teams my friend sent," he said to Remy.

"Good," he replied.

Bolan waved at Mott, then stepped out into the courtyard as the rotors on the choppers slowly came to a stop. Several men moved forward to lend a hand to Remy and Rio. "Get them to a hospital," he said.

"Wait," both Remy and Rio said at the same time.

"I've got to move," he said. "Costello will be long gone if I don't get going."

"I know," Rio said. "I just wanted to thank you for coming for me."

"Anytime," Bolan said, then turned to Remy. "And thank you. When you're on the mend, I'll make sure that you know how to get in touch with a friend of mine. Maybe you can decide to be in the world again. You're a good soldier."

"Thanks, Cooper," Remy said. "Now go get that bastard."

"I'm on my way," he said, then turned and ran for his truck.

BOLAN GOT BACK to his SUV, jumped in and gunned the engine. By his best estimate, Costello probably had about a half-hour start, and maybe even a bit longer than that. By this point, he'd be almost back in the city and headed for the docks. It was the most logical place for him to go, especially if he wanted to salvage anything or get out of the country and into international waters. With a fast yacht or speedboat, he could be out of U.S. jurisdiction within an hour, perhaps less.

Not that jurisdiction would stop the Executioner, but it would complicate things if Costello got out to sea, even just making it difficult to find him. That thought was enough for Bolan to increase his speed even more. He hit the highway that led back into the city at seventy miles an hour, and began weaving through traffic. His eyes were focused on the vehicles in front of him, so the sudden wrenching as he was rammed from behind was startling. His back window shattered, spraying safety glass into the passenger compartment and out onto the road.

He yanked on the wheel, tires screeching, and checked his review mirror. Behind him, two heavy duty pickup trucks with police decals were closing in on him once more. Bolan floored the accelerator and the big SUV engine growled as he shot forward, dodging into the left lane and getting in front of the two trucks before they could cut him off.

Other drivers laid on their horns in irritation as he raced down the highway, several times brushing up against another vehicle or the concrete divider as he switched lanes to try to keep the two trucks behind him. Fortune appeared to be against him, however, when up ahead he saw several semis taking up both lanes. He'd hoped to find a good place to get off the highway and onto a side road, but it looked like his time was up.

Rather than slow, he actually forced the gas pedal to the floor, trying to gain a little more room. He couldn't go to the left—the divider was easily four or five feet high, and the lanes weren't wide enough for any kind of maneuver between the semis, especially the large tanker hauling tandem, so he steered to the right. The shoulder was rough and slowed him somewhat, but he knew it would have an effect on his pursuers as well.

The two pickups closed in behind him and were blocking him in, one behind him and one in the left lane. Bolan narrowed the gap between himself and the semi in the right-hand lane, coming up almost to his bumper. As the closer pickup tried to ram his back end, Bolan yanked the wheel hard to the left, smashing into the pickup in that lane, while letting the other one get beside him on the right.

The sound of breaking glass and tearing metal filled the air.

He yanked the wheel back to the right, forcing that pickup off the road and into a water-filled ditch. The truck on his left smashed back into Bolan, trying to force him off the road as he'd done to the other vehicle. Bolan finally got a look at the person driving and was stunned to see it was none other than the Chief of Police Duke Lacroix.

His eyes were wide and mad, his mouth open in a strange, haunting grin. It appeared that the man had gone completely over the edge.

Bolan fought to keep the SUV on the road, and waited for Lacroix to try to ram him again. This time when the chief moved in, Bolan slammed on his brakes. The thrum of the antilock braking system pushed against his foot, but he fought it as hard as he could. The smell of burning rubber filled the air, and Lacroix's pickup shot into the gap in front of the SUV.

The Executioner didn't hesitate but immediately floored the accelerator. The SUV leaped forward, engine revving, and slammed into the tailgate of the pickup. Bolan could see Lacroix's right arm waving angrily, but the warrior didn't back off. In fact, he kept his foot on the gas, pushing the pickup more and more into the narrow space of shoulder between the semi and the edge of the road.

Looking through the cracks in his own windshield and through the front of Lacroix's, Bolan saw what he'd been hoping to see: a large concrete piling used to hold up an overpass. Lacroix had to have seen it, too, because he suddenly slammed on his brakes. But Bolan kept his foot to the floor, and the semi started to pull ahead.

He glanced once more through the windshield and saw Lacroix pointing his gun out the window. The chief began to fire wildly, and Bolan leaned down near the dash, leaving himself just enough visibility to see.

Bolan mentally counted down, then stomped on the SUV's brakes. The seat belt cut into his shoulder and pelvis as his bumper disengaged from the pickup. Tires shrieked as they closed in on the pillar. Bolan stopped just in time, but Lacroix's vehicle didn't have enough room to make the stop and it ran into the concrete column going about forty miles an hour. The front end of the truck exploded, and Bolan could see the air bags detonate and fill the compartment with the silvery-gray powder they contained.

The Executioner parked on the side of the road, got out of his vehicle and walked forward. The pickup's driver's door sprang open and Lacroix fell out of the seat. Somehow he got to his feet, but he was a walking mess. One eye was a bloody hole, and his left arm hung loosely, the skin shredded and the bones exposed. He dragged his right leg behind him, and Bolan could see that it was twisted at the knee. Bright bloody froth ran from his mouth, which typically meant internal bleeding.

He should've been dead, but he wasn't, and as he brought his pistol to bear, Bolan realized it didn't matter to Lacroix in the least what *should* be. The soldier drew his Desert Eagle and fired once, taking off the top of the man's skull just above the eyebrows. Lacroix flew backward, and when he landed he twitched once, then was still.

Tired and aching, Bolan got back in his battered SUV,

thankful that it was still in working condition. If he hurried, he might be able to catch up with Costello and put the last player in this game out of the way for good.

20

There was little point in a stealthy approach to Costello's warehouses on the docks. As Bolan pulled up on the street outside, he could hear muted pops of gunfire from inside. In addition to his own SUV, there were a number of other vehicles parked on the streets, which appeared to be out of the norm for the area: a Hummer, four silver Mercedes Maybachs, a handful of black BMW sedans and a custom-painted Cadillac Escalade. Most of the plates were from out of state. Unless the wages had really gone up in this part of the world, none of these belonged to the dockworkers.

Bolan moved to the back of the SUV and got fresh magazines for the two Desert Eagles he was carrying and dumped everything he didn't need. As far as he was concerned, his only interest here was in finding Nick Costello, aka Nikolai Agron, and putting him in the ground. Once that was done, he could get back to his life and whatever mission came next.

Random shots continued in the closest warehouse, and Bolan decided to start there. He jogged across the street, noting on his way by that the guard shack was empty, then to the door that he'd used when Sandra had first brought him here. The shots were louder now, and he eased open the door and slipped inside, using the surrounding shadows and crates as cover.

Above him, men ran along the catwalk, diving in and out of offices and behind stacks of boxes as they took potshots at one another. Based on the shouting, it was a virtual melting pot up there—Israelis, Russians and Italians trading shots. Apparently none of the combatants had any sense of who was who, only that all hell had broken loose and they'd been sent here to stop it.

Bolan had no real interest in these men, and wanted to avoid them if at all possible. If he were to guess, the Israelis had more manpower in place and better equipment—no doubt some of it their own recaptured from this very warehouse. He moved along a narrow row of crates, trying to get a better position to see the far end of the catwalk. That would be where the biggest office was located.

His eyes were looking up, keeping watch on the ongoing battle above his head, which almost prevented him from seeing the man coming up behind him. Only a barely noticeable change in the shadows on the stacks of crates ahead gave the Executioner any warning at all. He dived forward just as the crowbar came crashing down toward his head. The sharp spike on the end grazed the back of his skull and raked a path down between his shoulder blades.

Rolling, Bolan kept moving, trying to put some distance between himself and his attacker. He got to his feet and saw that the man was closing fast, still clutching his crowbar.

"Time to die," his adversary said, and Bolan marked the accent as Russian.

"Not today," Bolan said. "I'm busy." He took another step back and moved to one side as the crowbar came at him again.

The man overextended, and his momentum carried the full length of the weapon past its target. Bolan snapped out a kick at his wrist and caught the man directly on the protruding end of his ulna, breaking it. The Russian yelled out in pain, dropped the crowbar and yanked his hand back, cradling it against his chest.

Bolan didn't give him time to consider his next move, but closed in rapidly, throwing hard jabs to the right side of his body, making it harder for him to block. The Russian kept moving away, but was tiring. Finally, Bolan dropped low and executed a leg sweep, knocking the man to the ground. Lunging forward to finish him, the warrior saw that there was no need. Blood was running from behind the man's head where he'd hit it on the concrete floor. He was out cold.

Returning his attention to the fight on the catwalk, it appeared to Bolan that the Israelis were getting the upper hand, pushing both groups back toward the stairs. The office he'd been looking for was dark, and Bolan decided to look in the other warehouse for Costello. He took a step in the direction of the door, when he saw a tiny movement out of the corner of his eye and stopped.

The door to the office had been closed, but now it was slightly ajar. Bolan pressed himself closer to the row of crates and crept forward, watching for additional movement. The door opened a bit more, and he glimpsed a hand as someone inside tried to assess the situation on the catwalk. Another pause, and then the door opened wide enough to allow three men to step through. One of them was Nick Costello. The other two were likely bodyguards. Considering how few men he had left, it was amazing he could spare two from the fight to protect his own precious skin.

They moved out single file, but didn't head in the direction of the fighting. Instead, they walked to the very edge of the catwalk and behind a stack of crates. Bolan peered into the heavy shadows there, but could see nothing.

"Damn," he muttered to himself, then he broke into a fast

jog, trying to get to the other side of the warehouse before Costello vanished again.

He managed to weave a path almost directly underneath where the catwalk ended, and looked up, but Costello and his men were gone. Not ready to give up, Bolan moved closer to the warehouse wall and finally noticed a narrow set of stairs that led down to his level. The nearest row of crates provided cover and a space just large enough for a man to walk through. Assuming that they hadn't gone past him in the maze of crates, they had to have gone that way. Bolan quickly set out after his quarry.

The narrow path followed the wall all the way to the far end of the warehouse, where a single door, standing ajar, led out to a concrete pad. Bolan slowed long enough to check that the way was clear, then went through the doorway. Forklifts were parked along the far side of the pad, and the next warehouse was dark and silent. Deciding quickly, Bolan made a beeline for the docks, suspecting that Costello had figured that it would be better to run and live than to stay and die.

He rounded the corner of the warehouse closest to the docks and saw the three men running down one of the long piers where private vessels were docked. Most of the boats there were miniyachts and speedboats. It would have been a tough shot, but Bolan silently wished he'd kept the Tavor assault rifle. Instead, he had no choice but to run after the escapees.

He hit the pier at full speed and had to have made enough noise for Costello to hear, because suddenly one of the bodyguards stopped and turned, drawing a weapon. Bolan hit the deck, pulling his own Desert Eagle and squeezing off a round.

Costello didn't slow by so much as a step. He just kept running with his last remaining man, while the other bodyguard opened fire with what sounded like a Glock 22, a .40-caliber handgun with a lot of stopping power. If he hadn't dropped to the ground, Bolan thought he'd probably be breathing through an extra hole in his chest right now.

As it was, his movement caused the man's first shot to go high. He adjusted and Bolan rolled to his left, firing his own weapon in an effort to force the man to change position. It worked, and he took cover behind hanging nets on a nearby post. This gave the Executioner time to get back to his feet and find cover of his own, ducking behind some wooden crates. It wasn't ideal, but it would have to do.

Ignoring the fleeing Costello for the moment, Bolan concentrated on his current enemy. The netting was a thick, heavy rope, with open squares. He watched carefully, hoping to see a contrasting color or movement behind it that would give him a target. Unfortunately, he couldn't see anything that would give away the other man's position. On the far end of the pier, a boat engine flared to life.

Costello was getting away—it was time to force the issue. Bolan adjusted his position slightly, then pushed over the top crate. It crashed down, splintering on the hard wood of the pier, but the Executioner kept his gaze on the netting. A single shot rang out before the shooter realized his mistake, but that was all Bolan needed.

He fired the Desert Eagle where he'd seen the brief flare from the other man's gun. There was a low grunt and a sigh, then a splash as Costello's man fell into the water below. Bolan took off, not bothering to stop and check the results of his shot. He could see a small yacht pulling away from the pier, and Bolan knew there was no way he'd get to it in time to stop it from leaving. To go after them, he'd need his own craft.

The Executioner chose a heavy looking speedboat to his left. Untying it from the cleats, he jumped in and headed for the driver's seat. There wasn't a key, and Bolan didn't want to waste time looking for one, so he simply popped open the ignition module and went to work with a small bladed penknife. It took a couple of minutes to get the wires identified, but it wasn't much different from hot-wiring a car. The engine roared to life, and Bolan put the vessel in reverse and began backing away from the pier.

The motor yacht Costello had taken was moving fast and heading for open water.

SNEAKING OUT of the office, Nick had spotted Bolan in the warehouse and cursed silently. The man was like some kind of killing machine, programmed to destroy everything Nick had built. Unfortunately, he was running out of men to throw at his adversary, and in a confrontation, Nick knew he was far more the kind of man to stab someone in the back than fight the person head-on. He'd run from the warehouse, hoping to get to the yacht before Cooper spotted him. Even then, luck wasn't on his side.

He'd heard Cooper hit the dock running, glanced back once and assigned one of his two remaining bodyguards to take him out. He'd kept an ear open as he jumped aboard and got the yacht running, listening to the shots exchanged. When it went quiet momentarily, he assumed the worst. At this point, it couldn't possibly pay to be an optimist.

Nick was headed toward open water when his last man, a good guy named Vegas who he'd hired straight out of PMC work in Africa, tapped him on the shoulder and pointed. A speedboat was pulling away from the pier. "He's not human," Nick muttered.

"What's that, boss?" Vegas asked.

"Nothing," he said. "He's persistent." Nick pointed to the main cabin. "There are weapons down below. Go and pick out something powerful and kill that crazy bastard, would you?"

"Sure thing," he said, and moved off to find a weapon.

Nick swore again, wishing he'd thought to put a bazooka down there, instead of just rifles and handguns. His chances were waning, he knew, and he pushed the throttle forward, mentally urging the boat to go faster.

A quiet voice deep inside his mind gibbered in fear, however, whispering that he could run to the ends of the Earth or down to the gates of hell, and when he got there, his pursuer would be waiting for him.

ONCE HE WAS PAST the end of the pier, Bolan pushed the throttle forward on the speedboat. Its twin engines roared to full life and the boat shot forward, cutting through the water like a shark. He was closing the distance on the yacht and had pulled into its wake, when the first shot crossed his bow and took out the window to his left.

Bolan yanked the wheel hard to the right. It was a challenge to steer the boat, chase the yacht and shoot back all at the same time. Another round came in, this one a little higher, making a high-pitched zing as it went past. An assault rifle, he thought, continuing the zigzag pattern with the boat to make targeting more difficult for the shooter. The good news, and there wasn't much of it, was that shooting from a moving platform like a yacht, at a moving target like a speedboat, was incredibly difficult, even for a gifted marksman. Another bullet went by, this one hitting the glass to Bolan's right.

He yanked the wheel again, contemplating his choices, and then reached a decision. He swiftly went out to the starboard side of the yacht, pushed the throttle all the way up and took an angle, aiming for the center of the yacht. There was no other way that he could see that would result in the outcome he wanted.

Bolan ducked behind the windscreen, keeping as low a profile as possible. Bullets came in at speed, breaking glass, cracking the hull and ricocheting off the deck. The shooter had seen what Bolan was doing and panicked, knowing that the yacht was the slower vessel.

Bolan risked a peek over the glass, gauged the distance and began counting down the numbers. When he hit three seconds out, he jumped up, took two running steps and jumped over the side, arching out into the water as far as he could get.

The horrendous crash echoed over the waves and down into the water. Bolan knew well enough not to surface right away. He slowly swam to the surface and saw that the speedboat had slammed into the side of the yacht and exploded on impact. Flames dripped down the sides of the hulls and wreckage floated on the water all around him.

Bolan began to swim closer and looked up in time to see Costello standing at the bow of the yacht, blood running from his face. He appeared dazed and confused and though his eyes passed right over Bolan's position in the water, nothing seemed to register.

The Executioner swam to the back of the yacht, found the ladder and climbed aboard. The body of the last shooter was on the deck, almost cut in two. He stepped over the corpse and made his way to the front of the vessel, where Costello still stood staring out into the Gulf, like a man looking for something he'd lost long ago.

"Costello," Bolan said, kicking a piece of fiberglass wreckage out of his way.

Nick turned in his direction, staring, but not saying anything—pointing a gun right at Bolan.

"Nikolai Agron," Bolan called, raising his voice. In the

distance, he could see the flashing lights of Coast Guard cutters heading their way.

For a moment, he thought the man had gone deaf in the explosion, but then he said, "You know me?"

Bolan nodded. "Yeah, I do." He moved closer. "Your name is Nikolai Agron, but here in New Orleans, you've been calling yourself Nick Costello."

"That's right," he said. "I've been Nick for so long, I have a hard time remembering that I was once Nikolai."

"The game is over," Bolan said. "You've lost, Nick."

"Call me Nikolai," he said. "Are you going to arrest me, Marshal Cooper, or whoever you really are?" He began to laugh, waving the gun around. "I know enough to make sure that I'll never go to prison, you know. Russian secrets, Israeli secrets, Mafia secrets." He laughed harder. "I'll still be rich, still be free, and maybe my next identity will be yours!"

"There's not going to be an arrest," Bolan said, watching the laughing man intently.

"You're already prepared to make me a deal?" the man laughed. "So soon?"

Bolan shook his head. "Yeah, I've got a deal for you."

"What?" the man asked, his eyes wild. "What's your best offer?"

"Death," Bolan said quietly.

Nick Costello laughed again, but this time he brought the gun up with control and aimed it directly at Bolan and began to squeeze the trigger.

Bolan already had the Desert Eagle free of its holster and squeezed the trigger twice. "It's better than you deserve."

In the long seconds it took for Nick's brain to register the giant holes in his chest, he stared at Bolan, his eyes suddenly sane. "That's fair," he gasped, then he collapsed onto the bow of the yacht, dead.

Bolan holstered his weapon, then leaned against the bow.

It wouldn't be more than a couple of minutes before the Coast Guard arrived, and while he had no intention of explaining anything, he knew that a ride back to shore would beat the hell out of swimming.

Epilogue

The sun filtered in through the hospital window, and the gentle warmth stirred Bolan from his vigil. He looked up and saw that Rio was awake. The surgery to save the marshal's leg had been successful, but the rehabilitation was going to be a long process. The leg was elevated and in a cast with a drain. Rio tried to reach down and rub it, and the look of consternation on his face when he couldn't quite reach was almost comical.

"If you think it itches now," Bolan said, "you're in for a long road."

Rio grinned. The swelling was worse on the left side of his face, which made his grin somewhat lopsided, and Bolan could see that he had difficulty opening that eye. There was a fine line of stitches above his right brow, and he sported more on various parts of his body, especially his legs.

"You're here," Rio said, his voice dry and rough. Bolan stood up to get him some water from the cup on the table. "That must mean that you got Costello or Agron or whatever the hell his name is."

"Was," Bolan corrected softly. "Whatever his name was. I'm sure they'll get it right in hell, but the important thing is that his days of causing trouble here are over."

Rio held out the hand that didn't have an IV drip in it. "Thank you, Cooper. I owe you my life."

Bolan took the proffered hand and shook it firmly. "I won't say it's my pleasure, but I'm glad I was able to help."

The soldier heard footsteps approaching and looked up to see Remy's frame filling the doorway. The bandage on the man's shoulder was heavy and white. He'd needed minor surgery to get the bullet out and repair the vessels, but everything had gone well and he was healing quickly.

"I don't think we've officially met," Rio said. "I'm the dumb-ass who got kidnapped by a phony mafioso and almost got the lot of us killed."

Rio held out his hand from the bed. Remy moved closer, waving the marshal back onto the pillow.

"Remy. And don't you trouble yourself none. I haven't had that much action in a while. Makes a man remember what he's capable of. It felt good to be useful again."

"Speaking of useful," Bolan said, digging into his pocket and pulling out a business card. He handed it to Remy.

"That's Hal Brognola's direct line. He's a contact. He's also the one that put us in touch with Grady Black, made sure supplies got here and generally pulled our fat out of the proverbial fire."

"I don't know…" Remy rumbled, his voice trailing off.

Bolan held up his hand. "Look, you can fade into the background and no one would blame you, but you're talented and a good soldier. I'd work with you anytime. I told Hal that you might give him a call. If not, that's okay, too. You can decide when you're ready, but the choice isn't as hard as you might think."

"How's that?" Remy asked.

Bolan shrugged. "Have a life and make a difference to the world, or don't." He offered his hand to the big man, and they shook on it.

The soldier stood and moved to the door.

"Where are you going?" Rio asked.

"I have one more patient to visit. Remy will make sure you stay out of trouble."

BOLAN WATCHED as the ICU nurse changed out the IV bag for Sandra Rousseau. They had been able to take her off the ventilator the night before, which was a good sign, but she still had a long way to go. He walked over to the bed and she turned to look at him.

"You look like an avenging angel standing there."

"I'm no angel, Sandra. I never claimed to be."

She closed her eyes and smiled. Bolan could see that sleep was tugging at her as her body was trying to heal. They had resuscitated her in the ambulance, and then she'd tried to die on the table, but the team worked through it and they thought she was past the worst of it.

"What can I do for you, Marshal Cooper?"

"I came to apologize," he said.

"For what?"

"I was supposed to keep you safe. You got shot and almost died. I should have been more careful."

"You weren't responsible for the choices that I made, but I kind of wish you had just let me die. I don't know that I want to spend the rest of my days in a jail cell."

"Well, I had some people speak with the prosecutor and the U.S. Marshals' office. If you're willing to help with the case, they'll get you a free pass. You can start over somewhere."

"Why would you do that for me?" she asked. "After everything I've done?"

He thought about it for a moment, then said, "Because some people need a second chance, maybe need it more than they even know. You almost died proving you deserved one."

Her eyes clouded with tears at his words, but Bolan didn't stay any longer. He clasped her hand lightly, then left the room and headed for the elevators. He didn't stop by Rio's room. Remy had plenty to think about. He'd said and done everything he could for all of them.

Time to go.

* * * * *

Don Pendleton's Mack Bolan

Grave Mercy

An evil regime returns to unleash terror across the Caribbean

The horror of the Ton Ton Macoute has returned. This Haitian madman commands an army of machete-wielding hordes, stripped of their humanity by powerful toxins, and he's plotting a brutal invasion. Now the zealot is about to experience the Executioner's trademark version of hellfire — righteous, hardcore and everlasting.

Available September wherever books are sold.

TAKE 'EM FREE

2 action-packed novels plus a mystery bonus

NO RISK

NO OBLIGATION TO BUY

The Executioner

Don Pendleton's®

STAND DOWN

A drug lord takes control of a Midwest town…

When a prominent family is murdered and their teenage daughter goes missing, Mack Bolan discovers an industrial meth lab functioning under the guise of a pharmaceutical company. A Mexican drug lord has taken control in town and the Executioner decides to shut down the lab…and clean up the town for good.

Available August wherever books are sold.

GOLD EAGLE®